It's the trial of the century in a 1940s North Carolina town.

Rape. Murder. Vigilante justice.

War hero and law student Wes Ross has to save his uncle—but hide the truth.

Taught to shoot in the rough logging camps of the North Carolina swamps, Wes Ross remembers his lessons well. Dodging hostile gunfire with dozens of other young Marines, he storms a remote Pacific island as one of Carlson's Raiders. It was the first commando-style attack of World War II. He blasts several Japanese snipers from their palm tree hideouts with buckshot before an enemy bullet sends him home.

The Carolina home front includes a new girlfriend and a new occupation, learning to be a rural lawyer in his uncle's law office, including courtroom intrigue and what goes on behind the scenes. Wes, like his uncles, is a good man, the kind who takes up for the poor and downtrodden, looking out for the black farmers and others who are easy prey for bullies.

Frog Cutshaw is the storekeeper in the Caney Fork backwoods, a swaggering ex-moonshiner who is deadly with his ever-present .45 auto pistol. Frog's daylight rape of a married woman and the brutal killing of her husband bring on Bible Belt vigilante justice, an eye for an eye, life for a life.

Wes is caught in the middle as a participant in the killing of Frog Cutshaw. Soon, one uncle is being tried for a murder he planned but did not commit, and another uncle defends him, but circumstances and witnesses threaten to convict the wrong man.

Wes knows all too well who pulled the trigger of the 12 gauge pump gun and knows that the shooter could end up on Death Row.

Murder in Caney Fork

by

Wally Avett

Bell Bridge Books

This is a work of fiction. Names, characters, places and incidents are either the products of the author's imagination or are used fictitiously. Any resemblance to actual persons (living or dead), events or locations is entirely coincidental.

Bell Bridge Books
PO BOX 300921
Memphis, TN 38130
Print ISBN: 978-1-61194-416-7

Bell Bridge Books is an Imprint of BelleBooks, Inc.

Copyright © 2014 by Wally Avett

Printed and bound in the United States of America.

We at BelleBooks enjoy hearing from readers.
Visit our websites
BelleBooks.com
BellBridgeBooks.com.

10 9 8 7 6 5 4 3 2 1

Cover design: Debra Dixon
Interior design: Hank Smith
Photo/Art credits:
Woman (manipulated) © Tadasp | Dreamstime.com
Texture (manipulated) © David M. Schrader | Dreamstime.com

:Lcmf:01:

Dedication

To my loving wife who has always believed in me, even after she has heard my stories many, many times.

One

1942

THE METAL FLOOR vibrated beneath our feet with the constant turning of the submarine's engines. Other Marines sat humped on the floor all around me, packed like sardines in space usually taken by torpedoes.

Ninety gung-ho Marines were there on the Nautilus, another hundred and twenty on the Argonaut, running somewhere beneath the surface nearby. Stuffed in these steel tubes on top of the regular Navy sub crew, two days out of Pearl and headed west a thousand miles to bring smoking hell on the Japs at Makin Island. Couldn't see the sun, couldn't see where we were going, it was almost unreal. So we talked, for endless hours, to pass the time and forget the dangers.

As a Southerner from a family of lawyers, I was a natural-born storyteller.

"Turkey Jack lives with a Geechee woman, on the very edge of the Big Carver Swamp. Because nobody is brave enough to actually live inside the swamp," I added. "Nothing in there but cottonmouth moccasins and mosquitoes. Scary place, even in daylight."

"I never seen a swamp," the boy from Maine said. "In fact I never seen the South 'til Parris Island."

"Well, Parris was okay but it's not the whole South. Turkey Jack taught me how to shoot."

"Yeah, I was around him a lot. My daddy and Turkey Jack were always big buddies and they logged a lot when I was growing up. We'd live in a rough camp way back in the woods, cutting down trees and dragging 'em out with horses."

"Yeah, I seen a lot of timber cut up in Maine."

"They taught me how to shoot better'n anything they taught me at Parris Island."

"What in hell is a Geechee?" Maine asked.

I had to remember to be patient with this Yankee. They didn't know much. I slowly explained that a Geechee is a colored person who doesn't speak plain English but rather a chopped-up sing-song language with lots of strange words. Supposed to come from some islands down off Savannah.

Suddenly Maine asked, "Are you scared about the fight?"

"Naw, it'll come soon enough."

To tell the truth, I wasn't really scared about the battle. I didn't even think much about it. It was the adventure of the war I was interested in. Going places, seeing things I'd never seen before. I grew up in a little county seat town in Eastern North Carolina and Mama died when I was twelve. Daddy and Turkey Jack raised me the rest of the way. Then a big cypress fell the wrong way on Dad, and it killed him.

"So you don't have any parents, any brothers or sisters?" Maine asked.

"That's right, nobody left but some aunts and uncles and ol' Turkey Jack."

It was hot. The smells of the place were about what you'd expect—the scent of sweating men in close quarters, and oil and moldy clothes and all that. We had to take turns eating when it was mealtime, but thankfully they put the thing on the surface and let us exercise and walk around a little each day.

"Come along men, let's promenade on the grand deck."

We had to smile at that. The speaker was another North Carolina boy, a real hillbilly from way back in the mountains. Cornball sense of humor, and we all liked him for his jokes. Hillbilly led us up the ladder so we could all stand and stretch on the little deck. There was a cannon there. I figured the salt water probably didn't do it any good.

It was late in the afternoon and we were alone in the middle of the big blue Pacific with the big blue sky all around us, nothing to see but water and sky in any direction. It had been like this since we left Pearl Harbor.

That's what I mean about getting to see places and do things. Pearl Harbor hadn't meant a thing to me, just a name, when the Japs hit it last December. It was a big thing, don't get me wrong, but it was just a name. A strange name, like Hawaii.

After Dad got killed, I had floundered around for a while not knowing what to do. I spent some time out in the country with my Uncle Jubal and Aunt Alma. She's my dad's sister. And I lived mostly right there in Carverville with my Uncle Herman, my mama's brother, who is the biggest lawyer in White County.

"So, Flatlander, when the big war come along, you just had to join it, right?" Hillbilly said, grinning like a possum, full of piss and vinegar, as my daddy used to say.

"You got it right, mountain man. I was afraid you'd kill all the Japs and not leave any for me."

"Well, you just stick close to me when the blood starts a-flying and you'll damn sure see some Japs shot plumb to pieces. Mister, my gun is gonna do some talking."

Back in the hold, we rode into the night, not knowing really what time of day or night except by the clock. Hillbilly lay on a sleeping bag jammed in close to Maine and me and we all talked. He told us of the remote mountain county where he lived, named for the Cherokee, and we laughed at his stories of moonshine whiskey.

"I wisht I had a horn o' white likker right now," he said.

"Our Indians were about gone in the eastern end of the state," I said. Some of the Indian blood had been mixed with the white and colored people and we had those who were combinations of all three races. My friend Turkey Jack was one, mostly Indian but with both white and colored mixed in too.

"He taught me how to shoot when I was a kid," I said to Hillbilly. "I was telling ol' Maine here about it earlier. He told me better than the instructors at Parris."

"How'd he say to do it?"

Turkey Jack lived with a coal-black Geechee woman, a towering colored woman whose speech I rarely comprehended, in a one-room shack at Big Carver Swamp.

The so-called "big carver" had been a nameless Indian, last

of his breed, who supposedly lived alone deep inside the swamp and came to town infrequently to trade his carvings for salt and stuff at the stores.

The white people had named the mysterious swamp for him while he was still alive. And shortly after his death, to settle a big public uproar which involved the names of several citizens vying for the honor, had likewise named the town for the carver, Carverville. But I didn't think the Marines would care for that story so I didn't tell it.

"What did he say, Flatlander? What's the secret?"

"Forget the sight . . . bring the stock right up under your cheekbone . . . hold your face tight against the gun and shoot with both your eyes wide open. That way whatever you're looking at is your target, automatically. Pull the trigger and you'll hit whatever you're looking at."

"Both eyes open, huh?"

"Yep, that's all there is to it."

Hillbilly was lying against the little rubber boats, all folded up nice and neat, that we'd use to reach the island. They smelled too, a funny odor from the rubber and the waterproofing, I guess. I'd been around boats. Anybody from the Cape Fear country would know something about boats. But I never saw one you blew up with air to give it a shape.

Like the boy from Maine, our captain was a Yankee too, lots older than us. We were just overgrown boys, about eighteen years old, but he was a mature man. His name was Carlson and he smoked a pipe. He was the one who trained us, told us all about guerilla fighting.

"How about Roosevelt?" Maine said. "You'd think he would be in Washington. Not with us."

Hillbilly cackled with laughter at that. "Them damn Roosevelts are unpredictable for sure. His old daddy has dammed up the rivers out where I live, give people electricity even way out in the country."

Language had begun to fascinate me, in what I heard from Maine and in Hillbilly's drawl, which was really not as slow as mine. He spoke like the mountain folks, not as drawn-out as

East Carolina. And I noticed he said "you'uns" a lot too, in places where we naturally said "y'all."

"My grandpa Dockery always calls him 'that dam Roosevelt' and says he ain't saying a bad word cause Roosevelt built so many dams," Hillbilly said, laughing at his own joke. "My grandpa Dockery is a yellow dog Republican."

"What's that?" Maine asked.

"That's a feller that would vote for a yellow dog if the dog was running on the Republican ticket."

Most people pronounced Roosevelt so the first part of the name rhymed with "rose." But Hillbilly said it so the first part sounded like "ruse." I noticed he talked about some sort of fierce wild hog that roamed his home mountains too and he called it a "rooshun." It was some time before we got out of him that these hogs had been imported from Russia.

James Roosevelt, the President's son, was going with us on this raid. None of us knew him very well, but he was second in command to Carlson and we knew he was important. A tough Marine sergeant was his personal bodyguard and carried two Colt .45 automatics, one holstered on each hip. The scuttlebutt was that his orders were to shoot Roosevelt if he were in danger of being captured by the Japs.

Hillbilly spent a large amount of time sharpening and re-sharpening his Marine-issue belt knife, honing it on a little whetrock he carried. He would test it on his shin, shaving off leg hairs to prove its fine edge. He seemed skilled at this, and seemed to enjoy it, so I gave him mine to sharpen, too.

"What does yore Indian friend—the one that taught you to shoot—what does he say about knives?" Hillbilly asked.

I told him, "Turkey Jack had no use for a knife, contrary to the fact that most white people believed most dark-skinned men all carried knives and razors for self-defense." I told them about Turkey Jack fighting three drunk loggers at a bootlegger's shack in the swamps, all three of his assailants armed with deadly hawkbill knives. Turkey Jack had calmly picked up a hickory ax handle and whipped all three of them.

"Witnesses said he broke collarbones, he broke wrists, he

poked out eyes, and, as the last was falling, he brought down the butt of the ax handle on the man's exposed temple, killing him cleanly.

"The law wasted little time in the investigation and Turkey Jack was never even taken to the courthouse for questioning. The deputy sheriff sent to the scene pronounced it self-defense, just another killing.

"Turkey Jack always told me that if you had to use a knife, you've let an enemy get too close to you," I told them. "A knife is good for cutting up your food, that's all."

"Tell us another story," they said. They liked my stories, especially the ones with violence. "Shut up and go to sleep," I said. "We've got a long ride to go. And if you don't shut up and go to sleep," I chided them, "the Big Carver will come and get you. That's what my mama used to tell me—he'll come up dripping with water and mud from the swamp and carry you away."

"I don't believe in haints," Hillbilly said.

The boy from Maine just looked at us both—he didn't know what to think.

ABOUT A WEEK later, we finally got to Makin Island.

The two subs surfaced just off the beach of the island and we loaded out in the rubber boats with little gas engines and went in that way. We were all dressed in regular khaki that had been dyed black, to make us harder to see, Carlson said.

There was a mountain between us and the main settlement. We started around the shoulder of that mountain, easing through the trees and brush. It was about daylight.

I think they knew we were coming. We didn't surprise them, especially after a Marine let a gun fire accidentally. That whole morning was one big long rambling fight.

The Japs had snipers hidden in the tops of palm trees and they killed several of our men before we realized what their game was. I never did pray a lot, but I said a little prayer as we went in, asked the Good Lord to spare me if it was his will and make me strong and quick.

I was putting my faith in the Lord and that good Winchester 12 gauge pump the United States Marines had issued to me. Old Turkey Jack had taught me how to shoot a shotgun years ago and now my life would depend on it. It was loaded full with heavy buckshot and I could feel the weight of about a hundred shells I was carrying on me. I felt good.

Gunfire began to crackle constantly to the left and right of me as we walked into the Japs. Carlson was very informal in his methods and officers were right in with us enlisted men. We had little squads ranging here and there, taking on the Nips where we found them.

"Look at that," Maine yelled, pointing at a ragged charge by five or six Japs toward the left end of our line. The enemy soldiers yelled as they ran toward the Marines and a quick burst of fire put them down.

Hillbilly was off to my right, carrying his heavy gun at waist level, ready in an instant to level a horizontal burst into the bushes.

"I'm hit," he yelled.

I had heard a sharp crack and out of the corner of my eye, saw Hillbilly topple to his right, the muzzle of his automatic rifle pointing to the sky as he fell. Later, I would realize the sound I heard wasn't the report of the Jap sniper's rifle, but the flat impact sound of the slug bouncing off Hillbilly's steel helmet.

"Hold on, we're coming."

I didn't even think, just hollered to him and ran toward him. *Hillbilly, don't die on me.* I was talking to myself. It was all confusing. But in the middle of all that, all my senses on full alert, out of the side of my vision I saw movement in the top of a palm tree about twenty-five yards to my left.

"You sonuvabitch," I said calmly, and felt the pump gun coming to my cheek and shoulder. The front bead found the middle of that palm crown and I shot three rounds in about a second. There was a convulsion up there in the palm fronds and a little Jap soldier in dirty khakis tumbled out and fell like a sack of grain on the ground, his rifle still grasped in his hand

and his cap still on his head.

"Good shooting, man," Hillbilly said. Maine was helping him to his feet and he looked groggy but he was apparently all right. There was a fresh shiny crease on the side of his helmet where the bullet had hit at a shallow angle and deflected.

We walked over and kicked at the dead enemy, turning the corpse over on its back. I pulled my belt knife.

"You gonna scalp him, country boy?" Hillbilly asked, laughing.

"Naw, I just want to see what the buckshot did."

We cut the shirt off the Jap and he was a pitiful little wiry thing, probably didn't weigh much over a hundred pounds. There was an odor about him, rice and fish maybe, but his skin was clean. My three loads of buckshot had shredded his upper chest and he'd also caught a couple of big pellets in the head.

The boy from Maine got sick and had to puke in the bushes. Hillbilly gave him an odd look but didn't say anything. Then we walked on toward the settlement. There was sporadic shooting all around us.

Around the middle of the day, the Japs staged the only thing that looked like an organized battle. Not paying any attention to us, they formed a line and came toward us, several dozen of them advancing through the thin brush.

We had linked up with several other small fire squads and when the Japs got close, we let them have it with everything we had. There were Marines shooting guns, M-1s we had gotten from the Army, shotguns, Thompsons, old bolt-action Springfields, everything. We killed every one of the Japs.

I used the shotgun to ventilate the tops of any suspicious palm trees and you could tell they were learning about buckshot. Several times in the distance, too far to shoot, we'd see snipers bailing out of their trees and running away.

The Japs had a little town there on the bay and we ran them out of it, shooting everything in sight. There were some natives, too, who were friendly to us. Then we saw what seemed to be artillery shells kicking up big sprays of water around a couple of Jap boats.

"Jimmy Roosevelt is up on the goddamn mountain," a sergeant told us. "He's spotting for the deck guns on the subs and they're shooting the shit out of this harbor. Look, look."

A shell from one of the unseen subs on the beach side of the island landed right in the middle of one of the boats, sending pieces of it high into the air. Soon, another shell hit a Jap flying boat, some sort of a funny-looking seaplane the enemy had there.

It was like a scene you'd imagine from hell, all the dead people and the shooting and the smoke and the noise. The Japs had a building we called Government House, sort of a combination headquarters place and hospital. We took the flag down, the Jap "meatball" rising sun thing, and it was along about then that I got shot.

"What's the matter?" Hillbilly asked.

"I been shot . . . in the ass."

Sure enough, one of their snipers shooting from way, way off, had popped one in my right cheek, low and deep. I never heard the gunfire, just felt a sudden push and a warm burn spreading through my hip. When I felt back there, it was my own sticky blood soaking my leg.

Two Navy doctors had come from the subs with us and one of them put some medicine on my wound. Even on a battlefield, you get kidded about the spot the bullet hit. I reckon a person's hind end is just naturally funny.

"Shot in the ass, huh?" the medic said. "That'll look great on your record, won't it?"

"By God, I wasn't running away."

"I know that," he said kindly. "You were standing out there watching them take down that flag, like everybody else, weren't you buddy?"

I nodded, but it hurt. Physically and emotionally. Here I had come halfway around the world, rode in submarines underneath the ocean and killed Japanese men on a jungle island, only to end up shot right in the ass, of all places.

The rest of it was a blur. There was a Jap plane that came over and strafed us, but it didn't amount to much. As the afternoon wore on, the pain from my wound got worse. My hip and leg got numb and I couldn't walk very good. Luckily, we'd killed all the Japs.

That night we tried to get back on the subs but the waves were running too high and the little outboard motors wouldn't work and some of us didn't make it aboard until the next day.

"I shore hate you got shot in the ass," Hillbilly said. "You probably saved my life, shooting that sniper out of the tree. Hell, he mighta shot me again if you hadn't got him."

"Well, us Carolina boys got to take care of each other."

"You need to go to the doctor," Maine said. "He's operating on Marines on their eating table. Here, we'll help you walk."

I told them to tell the Navy doctor I would wait until everybody else had been treated and then he could look at my ass. We waited for several hours while various wounded Marines were treated on that table.

Finally a submarine officer, a Hogan from Canton, Georgia, came to our end of the boat looking for me. He introduced himself and kidded me a little but I could tell he was concerned about all of us.

"Where's the tarheel that got shot in the tail?"

"Right here, sir, ready and willing."

"You Marines did a good job," he said, and told us that they'd already gotten word over the radio that Admiral Nimitz himself would be waiting on us when we got back to Pearl.

"Just help me get to the table, sir."

They laid me down on their dining table, just Hogan and the doc and me, in a small room. They pulled my pants down, stiff with blood and salt water from the rubber boat trip. Then the doc said, "This is going to be easy. It's not in too deep.

"There it is," he said, squeezing and bringing out a slug, which he tossed to Hogan. The Georgian was standing in the doorway, amused at the sight he was seeing.

"Gimme that," I told him. "I gave birth to it, and I want it for a souvenir."

Hogan grinned and handed over the Jap bullet. It looked to

be about a .25 caliber, only slightly deformed.

I limped back to my space at the end of the sub and showed my prize to Hillbilly and the solemn boy from Maine.

"One of these almost got into my brain," Hillbilly said, holding the bent bullet up for everyone to see.

"So that's what's wrong with you," hooted a kid from West Virginia, good-naturedly kidding him. "I wondered about you."

"Look who's talking, ridge runner." Ol' Hillbilly gave it right back to him.

The trip back to Pearl was a week or more, just like the front part except we didn't exercise much. I couldn't. The pain in my hip was like a toothache, a dull hurt that never quit. The Navy doc shot me full of morphine and I know my eyes must have been glazed, the way people looked at me.

We, the returning Marine raiders, stood on the little narrow decks of the two subs as they slid into the dock,.

"There's Nimitz," whispered the boy from Maine. "He's saluting us . . ."

They said our raid on Makin had helped the morale of the American people, showed the Japs we could surprise them. Medics helped me to a Navy ambulance and took all us wounded to the hospital. That's all we cared about.

Two

"SO THE BIG bold Marine got shot right in the ass?" She laughed as she kidded me, the blond nurse from Minnesota about my age.

"That's right, honey, lemme show you my scar."

"I've already seen it," she said, serious now." I've seen a lot since I went to work in this place."

"Yeah, I bet. I'll be glad to buy you a beer and cheer you up."

"No thanks, but I hope you feel better real soon."

She was the best-looking thing I had seen in a long time and every man on the ward wanted a date with her. But she was all business.

She would roll me over on my face, jerk my pajama pants down from the back and put some sort of ointment on my bare butt every day. It was embarrassing, but I got used to it.

"When do you get to go home?"

"I don't know," I told her, and I really didn't. The wound itself seemed to be healing slowly but deep down in the hip joint, things weren't normal at all. I limped badly when I tried to walk and there was still some pain.

I saw the eyes of the guys in the ward who lived on pain drugs, and I didn't want that, so I denied the pain, taking aspirin, and tried to think about other things.

I lost track of time after infection attacked. One morning, a Navy doc suggested amputation and I yelled and cursed at them to spare my leg and hip. The nurse said they were trying some new medicine on me to fight the infection.

Pumped full of the new medicines and the old friend morphine, I was placed aboard a ship for California and a larger hospital. There it seemed I slept more than ever, groggy from painkillers. And I dreamed of another war and cannon smoke and death in the dogwoods up in Virginia.

Dad had had an old relative who was a Confederate veteran, and I had heard his stories when I was around ten or twelve. Despite the Depression, the family still gathered several times a year for big reunions and I had simply been one of the clan. In battered T-models held together with wire and twine, they would gather at a scenic spot along the river and eat fried chicken and sing old hymns and tell old tales.

The old reb, bald as a boiled egg, would get us little boys together and tell us of the campaigns under Lee, the names of the battles like some melodic chant. Petersburg and Fredericksburg and this river and that crossroads. His eyes glinted bright and his bony finger would point at us and his tobacco-stained iron-gray mustache would quiver.

More than anything, we wanted to escape and play ball. But his intent stare and his horrific words held us spellbound.

"Gangrene," he would say and the word seemed to hold an awful power.

"The flesh rots before your very eyes and it eats a man up," he said, his glaring eyes fixed upon us like an Old Testament prophet with a vision. "They would cut off arms and legs to try to stave off the gangrene 'til they had a pile of 'em taller than a man."

I could see him in my dreams again and smell the fried chicken. And hear the terrible threat of gangrene, wondering if it now threatened me.

New drugs somehow saved me and by Christmas time, I was out of the woods. The wound was tender but it had finally healed, leaving me with an indentation like a dimple at the entry spot. I could walk, still limping, but there was almost no pain and every day I could feel the hip getting stronger.

"You'll probably wear off your shoe heel more on that right side," the Navy docs said. "But other than that, you should be all right. Don't put any more weight on it than you have to."

They assigned me to a Marine base there in California and I tried a piddling desk job for a week or two. But it wasn't what I wanted to do and my limp bothered my commanding officer. He conferred with doctors and I soon got a medical discharge.

"Going home, are you, soldier boy?" the old man on the train asked.

"Yes sir, I've done my duty, been wounded and declared unfit for military service."

"You don't say."

I told him briefly about the big fight at Makin Island. And how I would always limp from the Jap bullet that hit me.

"Where did you get shot, son?"

"In the hip," I said. "In the hip." I was tired of folks laughing about being shot in the ass. You don't have to tell everybody everything.

WELCOME HOME, WESLEY ROSS was what the paper banner said on the front porch at Uncle Herman's house in Carverville. It had to be the handiwork of Aunt Hilda—she always had an artistic flair and the lettering was hand-done but good, looked professional.

"Come on in, Junior, welcome home," Uncle Herman said, and hugged me around the shoulders. My dad had been John Wesley Ross, too. He had always gone by the first name and, to keep us from being called Big John and Little John, like they do in a lot of families, I had simply been called Wesley. 'Course, inside the family, I still got a lot of Junior, too.

"Wes, let me hug you too," Aunt Hilda said. "Come here, you look pretty good for a boy that's been halfway around the world and wounded, too."

She smelled like something good cooking in the kitchen, where she'd been before I arrived.

"What's that I smell? Smells good."

"I'm frying chicken, Wes, and biscuits and sweet potatoes. We want you to sit down to a home-cooked meal. I bet you missed my cooking, didn't you?"

Uncle Herman said a special blessing, thanking the Good Lord for bringing me home safe and sound, and I ate like a starving hound. Lord, I ate. It was good to be home.

"Son, you can live here with us as long as you want," Uncle Herman said. "But what are you gonna do? The war's over for you. Are you going back to college?"

"We were trying to remember, Wes, before you got here," Aunt Hilda said. "You went to the teachers' college up at Greenville about a year or so, didn't you, before you went to the Marines?"

I nodded, mouth full of her good fried chicken, slathering homemade butter on a hot biscuit. It seemed so long ago, the classes at the college.

They chattered away and I stuffed myself, at one point pouring chicken gravy on the sweet potatoes. Aunt Hilda's eyebrows went up a notch at that.

"Why, Wesley, I don't believe I've ever seen a person put gravy on sweet potatoes."

"Yes, ma'am, I like it that way. You ought to try it."

"I don't think so. But different people eat things in different ways and I suppose it's all right."

"In South Carolina, they eat sugar on rice," I said.

"Oh yes, son, and they eat sugar on grits, too. They consider grits and rice cereals and they just naturally put sugar on it."

Uncle Herman launched into a long explanation of a lawsuit he'd been involved in and some sort of a professor, a special witness they had called in to shore up their side of the argument. "I'd always heard that an expert is merely a sonuvabitch from out of town," he said, chuckling, and she blanched at his coarse language at her table. "Well sir, this man was a perfect example. Stayed in the hotel at our expense, drank our likker and ate our food and then charged us his regular fee on top of all that. And when we put him on the stand for his learned discourse, he really didn't help us very much."

They brought me up to date on what had happened in our little town while I was away—the courthouse gossip, the church gossip, who had died or married or moved away. Boys I had gone to high school with were all gone to the Army or the Navy, sent overseas, scattered to the four corners of the world it seemed.

"Oh, this one's gone to England and that one's in Norfolk and another one's learning to fly airplanes in California," she said. "Women are working just like men. Two of my cousins—women who had never worked before outside of the home—are making good money working at an airplane factory near Atlanta, Georgia. Do you want some pie, honey?"

The steaming apple pie, its thick syrupy filling reeking of cinnamon, filled my nostrils and my stomach too and I nearly had to be helped from the table. Aunt Hilda was beaming.

"Wes, let's go out on the porch so I can smoke," Uncle Herman said. "These women don't need us in here."

A young colored girl had appeared from the kitchen, bustling around the debris of the meal and assisting my aunt in clearing the table.

We sat in big cane-backed rocking chairs on Uncle Herman's front porch and surveyed the main street of Carverville, a scant two blocks from the courthouse and downtown. The scent of Aunt Hilda's azaleas wafted across the porch, mixing with the stench of Uncle Herman's fragrant Cuban cigar.

It was springtime in eastern North Carolina in 1943 and I was twenty-one years old with a full belly and my feet up on the porch railing. Life was pretty good.

"THAT'S ONE OF ya Uncle Herman's cars, ain't it?"

"Yeah, it is. He loaned it to me. It's sure good to see y'all again."

The Geechee woman smiled and didn't say anything, which was just as well since I rarely understood her. Turkey Jack had hugged me when I walked up to their shack.

"That's a '35 Dodge coupe, ain't it?" he asked, cutting a chew of tobacco with a pocketknife. "You want a chew?"

"Naw, I'm not using tobacco anymore."

"What, a man live in Carolina where they grow the best 'baccer in the world ain't gonna smoke er chew?"

I shook my head. I used to smoke cigarettes and he knew it,

but he forgave me instantly for this lapse, this mild insult to his hospitality.

"Well, I sure remember that fast Dodge coupe," he said, mumbling as he worked the wad of tobacco into his cheek. It was Cannonball or Black Maria or some such common plug-chew. I had tried it a time or two but chewing tobacco was hot to my tongue, like chili pepper, and besides, it was a nasty habit with all the spitting.

"I wuz working on a road-gang one time when that little car was brand-new, doing ninety days for fighting, 'bout eight or nine year ago. You remember?"

I started laughing then and he cackled and the Geechee woman giggled self-consciously, trying to hide her grin and snuffling into her hand.

"Lemme tell it . . . lemme tell it," Jack howled, tears of laughter flooding his eyes. "Oh, it was good."

I was thirteen years old that summer, staying a lot out at Caney Fork with my aunt and uncle on their farm, my dad's side of the family. Uncle Herman, from my mom's side, had driven his new Dodge coupe out to the farm to get me and bring me back to town.

"Oh, God, it was fifteen miles of dirt road from Carverville out to Caney Fork," Jack said, helpless with belly laughter. "It was crooked as a blacksnake, all loose gravel and here y'all come doing about a hundred mile an hour . . ."

Uncle Herman would have made a good race driver and a year later in the same coupe would actually outrun a small airplane on a five-mile straight up near Wadesboro. But Jack had never heard that story. He was telling about the chain gang.

"We wuz cleaning out a ditch line along the road. It was hot and dusty, right in the middle of one o' them big curves. Guard was standing in the middle of the road with his shotgun and he'd called us out of the ditches and tole us to rake some of the gravel into the ruts.

"You know how a gravel road ruts out where the tires run and it piles up in the middle. A road grader machine could do it real quick, but we wuz prisoners with hand tools, so he wuz making us do it. We wuz raking and scratching, making the road level again, when here y'all come."

I remembered it all too well. On our arrival back in town a few minutes later, I had run into the bushes and vomited, a kid puking his guts out, because I had been so scared we were going to wreck and die.

"Yore Uncle Herman had that big-motored Dodge coupe in a sideways slide, rocks and dust boiling up underneath it, that engine running wide open giving everything it had to give. We could tell in a second he won't gonna let off for nuthin.

"The guard helt on to his gun but he run like a skeered haint and we dropped every tool we had and scattered like a covey of quail."

In my mind I could still hear the sounds of the wooden shovel handles snapping and the metallic thuds of the tools impacting the sides and running boards of the flying car. Uncle Herman grinned and fought the wheel, maintaining the power slide until we hit the next straight and the little car plunged on toward the county seat.

"That guard cussed," Jack said, shaking his head and wiping his eyes. The Geechee woman was snorting like a horse, her upper body rocking back and forth in rhythm with the laughter. "He ranted and raved, said that damn lawyer ought to be under the county jailhouse 'sted of practicing law in the courthouse. He knowed who it was."

He was sitting on their bed, on a ragged patchwork quilt. She was standing and I was sitting on a cane-bottom wooden straight chair. Their house was just one big room, no partitions, with a big rock fireplace Turkey Jack had made himself, the stones daubed with mud. On the other side of the room was her makeshift kitchen and it actually had a wood-burning cook stove, the only thing visible that was actually a cut above pioneer days. She could have been forced to cook in the fireplace.

The floor was hard dirt, packed and smooth from foot traffic, and there was an outdoor privy I could see through the window. There were actually two windows, but the stovepipe for the cook stove had been routed through one of them, which cut down on the daylight allowed to enter the shack. I supposed they bathed in the nearby swamp whenever necessary.

"How long y'all been here?"

"I lived here in a tent for about ten years," Turkey Jack said, nodding toward the woman. We built this house about six year ago. Makes a nice place, don't it?"

She dropped her gaze and smiled, the house a compliment to her presence here with Jack, the obvious feminine influence that got him out of the tent.

"Y'all ever going to get electricity and running water?"

"Well, the water ain't no problem. We got a good spring and she draws a bucket ever' morning. You want a drink?"

"Naw, I just wondered."

"And the nearest power line is about a mile away. They'd probably want a lot of money to run it down through the woods to us. Then there'd be a bill to pay every month. We don't want it. She's got a kerosene lamp she uses sometimes but we mostly go to bed as soon as it gets dark and get up when it gets daylight. Works out purty good."

The conversation turned to logging, his occupation when he worked. Jack had labored in the woods for years with Dad, who had gotten most of the jobs for them. Dad knew everybody in the county and small jobs just seemed to come naturally to him. He kept track of the money, which was never plentiful, and apparently, in the years since he died, Turkey Jack Lowery had found slim pickings.

"Junior, do you see that ol' truck out there?" Jack asked me.

"Yeah, I do. That's the only truck I ever remember you having."

"Well, it's been a good one. But the motor's gone, throwed a rod. And tell the truth, it ain't worth fixing."

"How about the short dog?"

"It ain't running neither. We had a cold winter and the motor in it froze and busted down the side, won't hold water ner oil, ain't fit fer nothing." A "short dog" was a poor man's version of a tractor. It was a cobbled-up monstrosity built from a wrecked car stripped down to engine and chassis. For pulling power, it usually had two transmissions running the engine's power through a double set of gears which gave the lowest of low gears.

"Well, the ol' short dog pulls better than a team," I said. "Lot of folks got them. You never did like horses, did you?"

"Got to feed 'em all year round, they kick and bite and shit all over the place. I hate horses."

Then he hit me with it. I should have seen it coming, and I didn't mind. But that's just the way he was. He wasn't the type to write me a letter, although he could read and write, and I would have gladly agreed to a partnership earlier.

"Don't get me wrong, Junior, but I got an idea," he said, and his brown eyes looked right into mine. "Yore daddy is dead now almost three years, right?"

I nodded and the Geechee woman looked away, seeming embarrassed.

"Yore daddy's logging stuff has been sitting in the yard at yore house in Carverville ever since they buried him. Two good trucks and a fine tractor. I'm down right now but I know the business and I can find men to work. Lemme have them trucks and the tractor and me and you'll be partners."

Several folks had asked me about buying Dad's equipment after his funeral but I'd turned them down, preferring not to think about it. Maybe it was a memory of him, maybe it was something I just wanted to hold on to.

Now his old employee wanted to put them to use—it seemed like a natural thing to do. I grinned and nodded and Jack grabbed and shook my hand in a powerful grip.

"Junior, we'll do good. I'm proud to be working with you again."

He knew a little tract over in the next county, he said, that belonged to a widow woman and would give us a good start. The woman had a brother that had just gotten out of jail and needed a job, but was a good worker and could do mechanic work, too.

It was agreed that I would open a charge account at both the hardware store in Carverville, where he could get saws and stuff on credit, and at the biggest service station in town, where we could buy gas and oil on a monthly credit account.

"You been out to see yore folks at Caney Fork yet?" Jack asked.

No, I hadn't but I would probably do that tomorrow. Uncle Jubal and Aunt Alma had a big farm at Caney. She was my dad's sister, and I had lived out there some with them. They knew I was back from the Pacific but I hadn't paid a visit to them yet.

"I bet yore people out there ain't too happy about it, but there's a bad one running the store now out at Caney Fork. A real bad white man name of Frog Cutshaw. Big fat feller, got a big stomach hanging out over his britches in front, a .45 Army automatic in his hip pocket for everybody to see.

"He's got somebody in the Army that gets him shells for that pistol and he practices with it a lot. He's good, I'm telling you. I hear through the grapevine that he killed a little girl last week. You watch out for ol' Frog Cutshaw and that fast-shooting pistol, you hear me?"

Three

THE NEXT MORNING, I drove out to Caney Fork in Uncle Herman's coupe, smiling at the memories of the day we had scattered the road gang on this very same road in this same car.

Nothing had changed since my childhood as far as the road was concerned. It was still gravelled and dusty, the twin wheel grooves routed out into two ruts by the infrequent traffic. It was wide enough for two vehicles approaching each other to pass, but just barely.

Curves were plentiful, each one a delight to drive as the little Dodge would break traction on the loose gravel with the slightest nudge of the accelerator. I didn't meet a single car on the whole trip and was soon making it fishtail a little, sliding sideways on the turns, sending up a plume of dust and fine gravel and thrilled with the power of the car.

"Come here and let me hug you," Aunt Alma said.

"Aunt Alma, you're looking younger every day."

"Her hair won't turn gray, Wes, like mine has," Uncle Jubal said. "I'm looking older all the time and she holds her age better than I do." Chuckling now, and grasping my hand in his calloused farmer paw, he said, "But it don't matter. I like it, even if folks think I married a younger woman."

Tickled with the attention, Aunt Alma gave him a playful slap on the arm and led us to the front porch rockers. They were a hard-working couple who had spent a lifetime on this farm, so I knew that for them to sit down in the middle of the day meant my homecoming was truly something special.

"I'm surprised at y'all, sitting down during daylight. Don't want to keep you from work—you don't usually sit on the porch 'til after supper."

"We've got so much to tell you," Aunt Alma said. "Besides,

22

it rained yesterday and it's too wet for Jubal to plow. He can afford to sit and talk a little. And I'll fix dinner in a little, but first, I want to hear about the war."

So we talked. And talked some more.

They listened to the war on the radio, they said, and got to read the Sunday paper sometimes about it. There had been a big write-up in the paper about the Makin Island operation and Aunt Alma had saved a clipping for me. They wanted to hear all about it so I told them.

"We noticed you limping, son. Does it hurt?" Aunt Alma asked.

"No, not any more. Except I can tell when it's going to rain because my hip will let me know. I can't run like I used to, but I can walk pretty good and otherwise, I can live a normal life."

"If you can tell when it's gonna rain, you'll be handy to have around. We can use you for a weather man," my uncle said with a twinkle in his eye. "And you can live with that limp—I have all my life."

"That's right, Wes, look it that way. Jubal has worked hard all his life—he's raised cotton and tobacco and corn and hogs and everything. That short leg never held him down a bit."

Uncle Jubal had been born with one leg about two inches shorter than the other, or maybe born is not quite true, maybe he developed that way. Anyway, all his adult life he had been forced to wear a shoe with a real thick sole, special-built just for him, on his left foot. It gave him a particular gait—he rocked from side to side as he walked—but otherwise, he was a God-fearing, foot-washing Primitive Baptist deacon, as strong as a hickory stump. Without conscious thought about it, somehow I knew at that instant my leg injury and his disability had bound us even tighter together.

They put me in my old room there, upstairs at the front of the big house, in an old bed with an iron frame and head rail. I could lay there at night and hear the frogs and crickets and whippoorwills, just like it had been before the war. I stayed with them for nearly a week, just unwinding. The war seemed a long way off.

"Tell me about the new man over at the store," I said.

"Who told you about him?" Aunt Alma asked, eyeing me in a different way. "Who you been talking to?"

"Turkey Jack Lowery. He said y'all got a bad one over here on the Fork now."

Uncle Jubal pursed his lips and shook his head. I could tell he would be choosing his words carefully when he spoke. But Aunt Alma would tell her side first. She always did.

"Jubal and I never traded much at that store anyway. When old man Root had it, long years ago, everybody on Caney Fork went there a lot. Including us. Old Man Root was a good fellow, gave people credit so they could get their stuff on time, pay for it later. We all liked him, didn't we, Jubal?

"But over the years, we got to buying stuff in town. Went to town every Saturday, like lots of other country people, I guess. Got our stuff there and brought it home. Jubal got a big gas tank here at the farm which the oil company comes about once a month and fills up. So we got our gas here, we buy groceries in town, we didn't really have a need for the country store."

Uncle Jubal picked his teeth very thoughtfully with a big kitchen match, and you could tell he was preparing to deliver the main address after her preliminary remarks. It was a scene I had witnessed many times as a youth, right here at this dining room table.

"The Roots were good people," he said. He spoke slowly and often gave more history than necessary, telling us all about the background of a person. I could see that Aunt Alma wished he would get to the point and tell the dirt on Frog Cutshaw right now.

"They farmed like everybody else and ol' Frank Root owned and ran the store for probably twenty-five years. He died out and a stranger ran it for a while. This Frog Cutshaw got the store about two years ago, while you were in college away from here.

"The Cutshaws were a big farming family hereabouts back during slavery times. There's a place called the Cutshaw Branch over towards the county line, but they all moved away and gone 'til this one bought the store. He's changed a lot of things."

"I'll say he has. That girl—"

"Hush now, Aunt Alma, let me tell it so Wes can understand."

"Don't forget that poor girl. I just feel so sorry for her family."

Patiently, Uncle Jubal went back to his narrative about the social history of Caney Fork Creek and the rich bottom lands along the stream and the families that had supported generations from the land.

"There used to be a lot of cotton grown here, but of course the weevils have ruined the cotton farming," he said. "It's sad to see." Aunt Alma was obviously chomping at the bit to tell about Frog, her patience with her mate about exhausted. He glanced over at her and got back on the subject. "The Cutshaws had all moved away and the family had sorta gone downhill, over in the county next door to us."

"They turned into trash, if you want to know what I think."

"Now, Aunt Alma, hard times can hurt people."

I had to grin at them. They were like a team of good horses that pulled together through it all, except one was slower and one was made with a faster gait.

"The Cutshaws, I'd be sad to say, got into bootlegging," Uncle Jubal said. "You remember the stories of a few years ago, the fast boats and all?"

Certainly I did. Prohibition had impacted Eastern Carolina in odd ways. The Coast Guard enforced a three-mile limit offshore and the bootleggers got around it by bringing regular store-bought whiskey down from Canada in fishing boats. They were okay as long as they stayed three miles off the beach.

Transferring the load from the Canadian boat was the tricky part. The bootleggers had fast boats, hammered together in some backwoods barn, some of them with airplane engines from the First World War. They would outrun the Coast Guard, bring their load of whiskey up into some hidden tidal creek and offload it into trucks.

"They say this one drove one o' them boats," Uncle Jubal

said. "He come back here where his family used to be, a long time ago, and bought the store."

"He's real fat, too. Musta been skinny when he rode in the boat."

"Drove the boat, Alma, drove the boat. But he was probably a lot smaller than he is now."

"Tell about the girl."

"Well, there was this girl. About sixteen years old. She was trash herself, I reckon."

"She didn't have to die."

"Well, that's right, too. Frog don't have a wife and he's near thirty so he's running after this one or that one, whichever one's in heat."

"Jubal, don't talk about women like they were cows." Aunt Alma was coming to the defense of her gender and he winked at her, though I could tell he had been properly chastised.

"The girl was fast and loose, according to all reports, and Frog may be the one that got her pregnant. Or it may have been somebody else, there was several suspected."

Frog Cutshaw, they said, and a couple more of her lovers had downed the girl in the back of a car behind his store and tried to dig the baby out of her with a spoon and a piece of coat-hanger wire. Witnesses said she had bled badly and went to bed as soon as they took her home. She had swollen up, they said, and her family assumed it was due to the shameful pregnancy. When she could stand the pain no longer, her father had taken her to a doctor in town for treatment, but it was too late. The infection from the crude operation ended up killing her the first night in the hospital.

"Cutshaw and those boys murdered her," Aunt Alma said. "They took their pleasure from her and then they murdered her."

Uncle Jubal nodded in agreement, and added that nothing would be done about it. Witnesses wouldn't talk, afraid of Frog, and if that wasn't bad enough, it turned out that Frog was a cousin to the sheriff.

"Through the sheriff's mama's side," Aunt Alma said. "You

know she was a Hartley and two o' them Hartley brothers had married Cutshaws, so there was the tie right there."

"Well, is he a Democrat, too?"

"Wes, of course he's a Democrat," she said. "Everybody's a Democrat. We are, you are, the sheriff is a Democrat. We fight like cats and dogs in the primary, but then that's it. Why do you even ask?"

I told them that Frog seemed to be such an evil man I thought he might even be a Republican.

"No, he's a Democrat too," they said. "We don't have even a handful of Republicans in this whole county. They'd be run out of town."

"How about the niggers, do they vote Republican?"

"Wes, don't say 'niggers' in my house, please," Uncle Jubal said. "It's a word that white trash says all the time and it makes you sound trashy yourself. Say 'colored,' but don't say 'niggers.' It makes 'em mad and they sull up and won't work. And it hurts their feelings too. They got feelings like other folks."

Aunt Alma rolled her eyes and looked up at the ceiling. I could tell that she was sometimes amazed at the applications of Uncle Jubal's religion, but she didn't challenge him on that. She knew he would start quoting the Bible to her and argue his case.

"Wes, he says 'nigra' and he always has," she said. "He's a good Christian man and I'm proud of him. Don't always understand him, but I'm still proud o' my man."

I put this little exchange in my mental file on language, which seemed to be growing each day.

"Maybe God'll bleach them out white when they get to heaven," he offered, a practical solution to the problem.

"If there's a colored section in heaven, like there is at the theater, then God won't even have to bleach 'em out white, Jubal." Come to think of it, I had never heard Uncle Jubal use the word *nigger* in private conversation or anywhere else. My own daddy, the senior John Wesley Ross, worked in logging camps all my life and he used the word a lot. But never to their faces. He usually called them "boy," or, in the Eastern North Carolina version he actually pronounced it "bo." As in, "Hey, bo, get th' saw an' les go."

I had an English teacher at the college up at Greenville who had opened my eyes to observe things about the language, about the way we natives talked in Carolina and the Southern drawl and the various dialects. She was a big heavy meat-ax of a woman but with delicate tastes. She loved poetry and didn't have much success making us love it, but she taught us to appreciate the language itself and its differences. She could mimic a country man talking, take it to the extreme, and the whole class would die laughing. I think she was probably a frustrated actress.

"How many ice teas did you say you want?" she would say, in perfect imitation of a waitress to a take-out customer in a café.

"Ah sho wan fo tees," she would answer herself as one of our local farmers. "'Cuz ah got fo thusty boys out dere."

"And that's the way the white folks talk," she was fond of saying, as we howled in laughter at her perfect impersonation.

Thinking back, my daddy often called me bo, too. It was simple and often a term of affection—he called all males under the age of fifty bo, black or white.

I MET FROG Cutshaw in person, in the flesh as they say, a few days later. And there was a lot of flesh—he was a big red-faced fellow with a pot gut, like Turkey Jack said.

"That all you gon' buy today?" he asked, taking my money for the cold Coke I was purchasing. It was a hot day and I got thirsty driving into Caney Fork from Carverville.

"Yeah, that'll do it."

I had parked Uncle Herman's coupe at the side of the road in front of the store. There was a colored helper standing at the other end of the counter, his eyes on us, a fly swat in his hand. No other person in the store.

"Yore goddamn uncle thinks he's too fuckin' good to trade at my store," he said. His eyes looked red, the rage showing, reminded me of a pig.

"I don't know about that. You'd have to ask him."

"If I want to ask him, by God, I will. Him and some of his kin made a scene in here one day. I should have shot the whole damn bunch of 'em."

I could see the pearl-handled grip of a nickel-plated .45 auto sticking out of his rear pocket. Turkey Jack was right, his belly was too big to carry anything in his front pockets—wouldn't be able to get anything in or out under that flap of flesh.

"Hadn't heard about that."

"Well, yore Uncle Jubal and his brothers was running their shit-mouths about that damn girl that died. Said it was my fault. Said Caney Fork would be better off if I was dead. That's a threat, Mr. Marine. By God, we'll see who gets dead."

I didn't answer, just felt that cool calm coming over me, like in the big fight at Makin. When it comes, I can tell. Everything focused right on the action, what steps to take, where to hit. Things seem to go in slow motion and I can see every movement done by me or the enemy. If he went for the gun now, I would bust the glass Coke bottle over his head first and then reach for the barrel holding ax handles two feet to my left.

"You got shot in the ass, didn't you, Mr. Marine?"

"Yeah, I guess so. Japs didn't like me."

"Well, I don't like you either, or the mealy-mouthed bastards in yore family," he said, then motioned to the colored youth. "Bo, set them cans up."

"Come here," he said, "I wanna show you something that'll make you think twice about messing with me." I followed him outside, sensing that the threat had subsided. At least the physical part of it.

"You shoot a .45?" Frog asked.

"I'm not Sergeant York," I said.

"Don't get smart with me, soldier boy."

I qualified—"I'm not crazy about pistols."

"Well, you just watch this, goddamnit, and then you can tell the rest what's what."

The black had placed some quart oil cans on their sides about twenty feet away, in some weeds at the edge of the dirt parking lot. The ends of the cans faced us, each maybe five inches in diameter.

He drew the shiny .45 with his right hand—pretty slick

draw for a fat man—and fired at the cans. I drank my Coke and tried to look bored. He emptied the clip, hitting every one of the cans, not dead center, but he managed a hit on each one and turned to me with a smug look as he reloaded with a fresh magazine from his other hip pocket.

"Can you do as good, boy?"

"Could if I wanted to . . ."

"Well, it don't matter if you can or you cain't, you tell the rest of 'em I'll damn shore shoot their asses off if they mess with me. And you get yer goddamn ass off my store property and don't ever come back or I'll get you fer trespassing. You hear me?"

He was mad, clear through, but I could tell that he wasn't mad enough to shoot me right then. Without speaking, I turned and drove away.

Four

"WELL, OF ALL the nerve," Aunt Alma said. "Imagine that bully threatening you like that. Threatening all of us."

"We must have got him really riled up," Uncle Jubal said. "He's a sorry white man, that's for sure, and they always say that a real sorry white man is the worst of all, worse than colored, worse than Indian or Mexican or anything."

"He's even got Jubal mad at our preacher," Aunt Hilda said. "What?"

"He is, too. Ol' Frog gives our preacher some money. It's supposed to be going into a building fund, but I ain't too sure about that."

She said she thought the money was to make friends in the community, get the congregation of the Caney Fork Missionary Free Will Baptist Church to buy all their stuff at the store.

"We do need a new church. Our old one is getting rundown and the roof is always leaking," Uncle Jubal said. "But Alma is a little bit hard on our preacher. There's no evidence that any money is missing. He gives a good message and we need that."

"His wife wears two-tone high-heel shoes," Aunt Alma said in a low voice, almost a whisper. "Right in the church house. I'm telling you, two-tone."

I had to put my hand over my mouth on that one to cover my grin. Aunt Alma was really cranked up over the two-toned shoes and Frog had apparently corrupted the preacher, at least in my uncle's eyes, though he didn't want to admit it.

"Frog's land borders ours, you know," he said, changing the subject. "He's got a big hog operation on his side of the creek, or at least a big one for this neighborhood. The creek's the boundary line and there ain't no bridge so we don't trespass on each other's land."

Aunt Alma nodded. "You can smell them hogs sometimes, though thankfully it's not often. I tell Jubal we're lucky the wind don't blow this way very often."

"He's got a big boar hog, son. I'm telling you the truth, they say that thing weighs five-hundred pounds, white as paper and mean as a striped snake. It's got big tusks that stick out of its jaw like a wild hog. He calls it Big Boy."

Alma nodded. "He loves that thing, too. He's proud of Big Boy and all the little pigs that thing has fathered."

"I think maybe Frog thinks he sorta is a big boar hog his own self," Uncle Jubal said, gritting his teeth and looking up at the ceiling. "He wants to run everything around Caney Fork and be the big boss hog.

"Come on and go with me today," he said. "Some of the men from the church are going to fix up the roof on a house for a young couple over there next to the store."

I loaded a ladder and some tools on the back of his old truck and we went.

As the crow flies, Uncle Jubal's house was less than a mile across the wide creek bottom to the store. But the roads didn't run straight at all. Uncle Jubal's farm road from the house out to the main road was nearly a half-mile long, and his house couldn't be seen from the road. And once you got to the main road, you had to turn left and go about another half-mile to the little run-down house we were going to fix.

"It's in sight of the store, but I don't reckon ol' Frog will bother you," he said.

I didn't reply. I wasn't afraid of Frog.

"This young man was shot up in Europe somewhere. I don't know where, but he's just come home to his wife and they're gonna be living in this house, renting it from some of their family.

"The old house leaks pretty bad and some of the floor joists is rotted out. Our church has a men's brotherhood bunch that takes care of stuff like this."

Several other farm trucks pulled into the yard of the house, some of them Jubal's brothers and their sons. I was introduced all around, shook rough hands and nodded. They grinned and kidded me about my wound, but if I was Jubal's kin, that was really all that mattered.

Uncle Jubal took charge of the work, which seemed to be a natural occurrence—everybody took orders from him readily. He sent some of us younger ones up on the rusted tin roof to find the leak and fix it. We nailed in a piece of tin and daubed a generous amount of tar around the edges to stop any rain that might blow in. My companions took a long look then commented freely on the wife.

"I'd come home to her anytime."

"Me, too, look at them legs."

"Legs, hell, look at them tits."

The Army vet and his shapely wife were climbing out of an old T-Model Ford to come and inspect our repair job. But my young Baptist companions were more interested in the wife, just like my Marine raider brothers would have been. I had to grin. Some things didn't change.

The vet was small and dark-headed, had probably been wiry at one time, but now was obviously crippled from the shrapnel. His left arm was shriveled and he held it up near his chest most of the time. I was self-conscious about my limp, but his gait was lots worse than mine. Both of his legs had been hit and he lurched almost like a crab. But he was tough and he made it up the steps and into the house where Uncle Jubal and the other older men were putting a new floor in the kitchen.

"Three of these joists rotted out," they told him. "We put in new ones and now we're putting a floor down. It's rough-cut sawmill lumber, ain't been planed smooth, but if you're gonna use it for a kitchen again," —the vet nodded agreement—"then we'll come back and put some linoleum down over it and it won't make no difference about the rough boards."

There was a breeze blowing and the vet's wife, said her name was June, was wearing a thin cotton dress and not much more. It blew up over her knees a time or two and some of the young farm lads got agitated. Uncle Jubal scowled at us.

"June and me thank you men for doing this for us," the vet

said. "I kin barely drive a car, can't do much anymore, and we need this place to live. It's handy. We can walk to the store if we have to, it's got a good spring and a garden place. We kin get by here, but it needed fixin', and we both thank you very much."

They both went around and shook hands with every man there. Her hand was moist and soft and smooth and she looked us right in the face. Her eyes were brown and she had just a little bit of lipstick on.

On the ride back to the farm, Uncle Jubal didn't mention us leering at the veteran's wife. He had promised them that we would help them move into the house the next day. And we did.

"I bet you know what this is," the vet said directly to me. We had dragged in some hand-me-down furniture their families had donated. Most of the other Baptist brotherhood had left, the moving job completed.

The vet reached into the back of the T-Model, and produced a new-looking M-1 carbine from under a ragged quilt. A few of the raiders had carried little rifles like this, which they told us the Marine brass had gotten from the Army.

"I liberated this one when I come home," he said. "Kept it hid in a locker 'til they let me out of the hospital."

OFF AND ON, I stayed out at Caney Fork for about a month or so, eating Aunt Alma's cooking and getting strong and healthy. But after a while, it got boring—farm life is so predictable.

"You're going back to town?" Aunt Alma asked.

"Your cooking has made me well."

"You're just saying that."

"No, really it has. And I'll come back from time to time."

"Well, you can still call us on the phone." They were proud of the new telephone, a novelty in Caney Fork.

"Yeah, I keep forgetting that. 'Course, with the party line the way it is, if I call you, all the neighbors listen in."

Alma shrugged. "It's still a lot better than nothing. I tell Jubal that all the time. We can call for help if we need it."

"If the lines aren't down or the electricity is still on."

"Thunder and lightning storms come and go, they always have."

I packed up a few clothes and left after Uncle Jubal had gone to the fields. She was standing on the porch waving good-bye when I drove the Dodge coupe out of the sandy yard, like I was going back to the war or something. My hip ached—I could tell another of those storms was brewing up.

The long road back to Carverville gave me some time to think about what I wanted to do. The future stretched out in front of me like a long winding road, hopefully at least a paved road better than this dusty gravel one. I wanted to make sure I did the right things.

Turkey Jack Lowery and his logging crew had taken Dad's equipment out of the yard and our old house looked really lonely now. I swept it out, hung my clothes in the closets and threw out some of the trash that had accumulated in the yard. There was an old push mower in the shed and I oiled it up and attacked the ragged grass.

Downtown, I found the city hall and the electric department, got them to turn the power back on. Bought some groceries and put them in Dad's old refrigerator, which started humming again, just like old times.

I was sitting at the kitchen table, going through the mail, when Turkey Jack knocked on the back door.

"I seen your car here and hoped it wouldn't try to run over me today," he said, laughing and shaking his head at his own private joke.

"Naw, not today. But I did drive it over your favorite road this week coming back to town."

"I bet you got the bills there. We making any money?"

"I can't tell yet. We're starting to get billed for fuel and parts. The trucks going all right?"

"Yeah, they ain't been run in a while and we had a bunch of dried-up gaskets to replace, but they goin' fine now."

"Where we working now?"

"Big stand o' pine over near the crossroads."

He had a tally sheet he brought from his truck, in smudged pencil, but readable. It had the dates and the numbers of truckloads of pine logs his driver had hauled to the sawmill.

"Let me have this one," I told him, "and you start a fresh one from this date forward. I'll take this one to the sawmill and check it against their records and see if we can draw a payday to take care of some of these bills."

"I thought slavery times was supposed to be over with," the elderly man at the sawmill said. "They tell me you got a big gang o' coloreds cutting down the woods everywhere." I couldn't think of his name but I remembered him—everybody in the timber business knew me from my daddy's doings.

"You might be right. I'm trying to keep the books and Turkey Jack's doing the hiring. I don't know who he's got helping him."

"I'm just kidding, you know that. We've only seen a couple of colored drivers coming in here with the logs. They're like me, they got some age on 'em. With the war going on, young men are getting hard to find. White and colored is going off to the Army."

"I got Jack's tally sheet here. Let's check it against what you've got and see if we can't get a check. They're using Dad's old equipment and I got bills to pay."

He opened a ledger book and laid the grubby-looking tally sheet on his own page of carefully-inked entries. I never suspected him of cheating us on the books—they usually did that when they measured the length and diameter of the logs on our trucks with their scaling stick to determine the board feet on that load. The loggers always called it the "cheater stick."

The numbers of loads and the dates they were received compared well, identical to each other. He stated a rate they were paying per-thousand for pine and I agreed it was fair. I wanted to show his check to Jack before we cashed it. Expenses for fuel, repair parts on the trucks and labor for his crew would have to come out of the money before we could split the difference as partners.

"It's 'bout what I figgered," Jack said.

"Could we make more hauling to a mill at Wilmington?"

"I hope you got more sense than that."

"It's just a thought."

"We doing all right here. Too far to Wilmington, take too much fuel and too much of a man's time. We need to be putting trees on the ground and getting 'em out."

The money looked pretty good, he said, and if he could rustle up another able-bodied man or two, we could tackle bigger jobs. I put my part of it in the bank. It didn't take much for me to live on, and besides, I was starting on my new job.

Uncle Herman said he needed an investigator, a man who could talk to witnesses and check on jury members and find out what he needed to know to be an effective defense attorney in court. They had the small court about every week, the one where they tried cases in front of an old judge, no jury trials.

"Big court, our regular term of Superior Court, will be coming up in about two weeks," Uncle Herman said. "The little court is our bread and butter. We make operating expenses out of all those Saturday-night fighting and drinking cases, the wife-beating and the bad checks. But Superior Court is where we get into the big stuff and especially the civil lawsuits, where we can make some real money."

"What do you want me to do?"

"Well, you said one time you might want to make a lawyer . . ."

"Yeah, I'm giving it some thought."

"Well, while you're thinking about it, I can pay you about fifty dollars a week—and that's good money these days—to do a lot of work for me, and keep it confidential."

I had agreed and went right to work. Naturally, I continued to drive the car he had given me, but I lived in my old house and took my meals wherever I could. Conversations with Uncle Herman were a continuing course in the life and strategies of an active, politically-connected small-town lawyer.

"What do you know about that God-awful abortion that killed that girl out at Caney Fork?" he asked.

I shook my head. I only knew what I had heard.

"Frog Cutshaw is obviously guilty in that matter. And he has a lot of money," he said, propping his fancy shoes up on his big desk. "Her family has contacted me, wanting to know if they should sue, or, if criminal charges are brought, could they pay me to be a special prosecutor and help the district attorney work the case against Mr. Frog Cutshaw."

"Are they gonna charge him?"

"I've spoken with the district attorney and he doesn't seem to be very interested in this one."

I said, as politely as I could, that I didn't think the girl's family had any money. That without some money involved, I didn't see how Uncle Herman would get involved in the case.

"Well, Wes, you've got a lot to learn. All wealth is not measured in terms of folding money only. The girl's family is very upset over her death, which they blame solely on Mr. Frog Cutshaw. Even though some other younger men were probably involved too.

"And you're right about the money. They don't have much, but they do have land, son. And people give me land in lieu of money. Lord knows all the land I've got. Some of it is not the best, but it is all land, and I have actually bought very little of it. And, of course, if we got a criminal conviction, it would make it easier to proceed with a civil lawsuit.

"In the best of circumstances . . ." He drummed his fingertips against each other and looking up at the ceiling fan, in deep concentration, "in the best of circumstances, I could receive a clear and free deed to some of their land for acting as special prosecutor in the first trial, and then I would take the civil case on speculation, so to speak, and end up with about a third of the monetary judgment we pull out of Mr. By-God Frog Cutshaw."

"I can see that a lot of planning goes into these deals."

"Now, don't get uppity." He was laughing at me now. "As an officer of the court, I expect a lot of respect from folks. I just want you to know how things work. If you become a lawyer, you'll be right in the middle of it."

"The regular folks don't really have an idea what goes on in the courthouse, do they?"

"No, son, and it's better that they don't. The fees I charge are sometimes the closest thing to justice some of these birds ever see."

"What if they don't want to pay what you charge?"

"I'll sue their ass and they know it. I'll put a lien on their land, take a regular weekly chunk out of their wages, get hold of their bank account. I'm the attorney for the bank's board of directors and I can find out how much they've got in the bank, help 'em get a loan or keep the directors from making a loan to 'em."

There was more to being a lawyer, I could see, than I had originally thought. I had day dreamed about defending some poor devil with a big speech in front of a jury, some innocent man and helping him get free. But most of Uncle Herman's clients were not innocent. His lecture ended abruptly when he sent me out in the country to look at a highway job.

The State of North Carolina was in the progress business, even in wartime, and a highway was being built on the east side of Carverville. Uncle Herman said valuable farmland would be taken for the new road and he would be involved, no doubt, in several lawsuits. "Go look at the land," he said, "let's get familiar with the route and who will be involved." He gave me the name of a local highway foreman who had occasionally been arrested for drunk driving and defended in court, of course, by Uncle Herman.

I found the man at the highway offices, which were adjacent to the prison camp. We talked sitting in the Dodge coupe, looking out at a gun guard in khaki supervising about a dozen prisoners being loaded onto a truck.

"Y'all work a lot of chain gang boys, don't you?" I asked.

"Yeah, and if wasn't for your uncle, I'd've been out there with 'em a time or two I guess."

"I'm glad he could help you. No problem now?"

"I got religion, and my wife and my preacher, they're both helping me now to stay sober. But that stumphole whisky 'bout got me . . ."

"State's gonna build a new road?"

"Yeah . . . Herman sent you out here to find out about it?"

We needed a map, I told him, and a list of the landowners involved. He said he might get fired if they caught him giving out that kind of information. But added quickly that he could provide it in a day or two.

"You can copy it, trace it or something," he said. "But I'll sneak it out of the boss's office and let you see it. 'Course, you know if they can't get the right of way for it, the route could change a little."

I agreed to his conditions and he said we'd meet in a booth in the back of a café in Carverville the following Thursday. He looked nervous when he walked away from the car. I watched the last of the convicts being loaded onto the work truck. He was wearing leg irons and could only take short steps.

It gets very hot in Eastern North Carolina in the summertime and I drove back to town with all the windows open on the coupe, glad I wasn't working along a dusty gravel road under the watchful eye of a shotgun guard.

Or even in the hot woods with Turkey Jack Lowery. I remembered how stifling the heat could get around the backwoods logging camps, the men dipping a head rag into lukewarm water in some muddy slough, then tying it around their heads to cool just a little bit. I was operating now in the coolness of the big brick courthouse or the law offices with their electric ceiling fans or the wind blowing sixty miles an hour through the coupe. I was getting soft and I knew it.

"YOU NEED TO go over to the Clerk of Court's office," Uncle Herman said a few days later. "Big Court's coming and they'll have the jury list drawn. Get us a carbon copy—they'll have some on hand for attorneys. Then you can start digging into the folks on the list.

"It's my business to know something about each one of 'em. Some of 'em will get excused and some are probably dead and some moved away. But I want to have notes on every one we can get some information on. And if we get into a trial, we'll really dig out the goods on every one that actually gets put in the jury box."

I walked into the back door of the big brick courthouse, which stood on its own square of land right in the middle of the town. I was learning to look up deeds in the old bound books in the Register of Deeds office, like Uncle Herman showed me. But the deeds office so far had been the only one I knew.

The Clerk of Court's office was larger, I knew that, and very busy. I entered it and saw Darlene Akers for the first time. She was simply the prettiest girl I had ever seen. Period.

"Can I help you?" she asked.

I stared at her. I couldn't help it.

"Can I help you?" she asked again, a slight annoyance showing around her mouth.

I stammered, but I managed to make a reply. I told her who I was and that I needed a copy of the jury list for Big Court.

"We all know who you are," she said. "Carverville is a small town. Everybody knows everything, people talk. You were a Marine, weren't you?"

"Yes, ma'am, that's right."

"Don't call me ma'am, I'm not your mama."

"I know that." I couldn't help but laugh at her sass. "I was just trying to be polite."

"Why are you laughing at me?"

"I'm not laughing at you. I'm just amused that you're so sassy."

"You don't remember me from school, do you, Wesley Ross?"

"I believe I'd remember somebody as pretty as you. Must have gone to school somewhere else, not Carverville."

"I did so, too."

"When?"

"I was in the eighth grade when you graduated and went off to college."

And she added that she had seen me then with a preacher's daughter, which was true. But the preacher's family, including

41

the daughter, had moved away and I had gone to college. There had been a girl at college, too, but the war had taken me away and I had forgotten her name.

"So that would make you about eighteen years old now, wouldn't it, honey?" I asked. I could be sassy too.

"I don't see that my age is any of your business, Mr. Marine. And don't call me honey. I'm not a waitress in a café somewhere."

"I'll take you to a café sometime, buy you a cup of coffee."

"I don't drink coffee, thank you."

"Well, you need to start learning. Let me have that jury list, I need to be going."

I smiled at her and gave her a big obvious wink, and she slammed the list down on the counter, jerking her gaze away from mine so fast I bet it put a crick in her neck. I chuckled out the door. Her little temper put a fire in her green eyes that took my breath away.

I had almost reached the back door of the courthouse, walking down a cool marble hall, when I met Frog Cutshaw wearing a white shirt with a flowery-patterned tie draped over his big belly. The tie was amusing to see—looked like it was strangling him.

"I don't see that big pistol hanging out of your pocket today. You mustn't carry it when you come to town." I was feeling lively after the exchange with the girl, and had to taunt Frog verbally. It just felt like the right thing to do.

"You come back to my store and yore ass is mine." He hissed when he spoke, the droplets of saliva falling on the gaudy tie. "You and yore goddamn uncle."

"Nice talking to you," I said, laughing at his fury, and breezed out the door.

Uncle Herman grabbed the list when I got back to his office and asked if there was anything interesting going on over at the courthouse. I told him I saw a good-looking girl and Frog Cutshaw.

"Well, I know who the girl is," he said. "And Frog Cutshaw may be going to the courthouse just to see her."

Five

I WAS SOUND asleep in my own bed in my own house, minding my own business you might say, when the Carverville cops almost broke down my front door with their banging and shouting.

"Get up, bo, get y'r ass out here."

Clothed only in my underwear drawers, every window in the house open to let in the nighttime coolness, I stumbled through the darkness and managed to unlock the door.

"Get your pants on, you've got to come with us."

"Are y'all arresting me . . . ?"

"Why hell no, we ain't arresting you, dummy, yore uncle said you needed to see something."

They took me in their police car to a section of town where poor white folks lived in shanties, a place called Ramsey Hollow. The town's only other police car was parked in the weedy yard of one of the shanties, its headlights bathing the yard and house in blinding white light.

"What's that lying on the ground?" I asked.

"It's a dead man, what your uncle wants you to see."

If Uncle Herman somehow knew about this incident and wanted me on the scene, it was apparently all going to make sense . . . sometime in the future.

The chief of police, looking as sleepy and groggy as I was, grimly shook hands and introduced me to the coroner, a local doctor.

"Bo, don't step in the blood,." the chief said. "It's a mess, ain't it?"

Lying on its side in the weeds was the corpse of a dead white man, freshly killed. He looked to be about sixty-five years old, grizzled gray whiskers he hadn't shaved in several days. His eyes were closed and he lay in a fetal position with his bony butt exposed for all the world to see, the body clad only in an undershirt.

"Look at the cigarette, how it burnt down to the meat."

The old boy had been smoking a cigarette when he was stabbed and fell. The cigarette was still in his fingers, the gray ash over an inch long. Like the cop said, it had burned down until it met the flesh of the fingers.

"I'd say his heart pumped maybe three beats after the knife punctured it," the doctor said, writing something down in a notebook. "There's no need for us to call a coroner jury on this one. It's plain and simple."

Beside the body was a pool of blood that looked to be maybe four feet across. The doctor said it represented all the blood that had been in the body, pumped out by the heart as the man lay there and died instantly.

"Y'all find the knife?" the chief asked.

"No, sir. We got his woman and put her in jail right away. But we come back and we never found no knife."

The night officers said they had been contacted in person by one of the dead man's neighbors, who had walked to the police station to bring the news. The messenger was frequently in trouble for drunkenness and saw the killing as an opportunity to get in good with the law.

"He said what?" the chief asked.

"He said he was glad to be assisting the police," one of the night men said. "Then he asked us if he would get any pay for telling us about this."

The residents of Ramsey Hollow would do anything for a dollar, the chief said. And then they'd use that dollar to buy cheap moonshine liquor.

"That's what caused this killing," the night man said.

"What?"

"Yeah, ol' Barney that come and told us, he said this dead one and his old woman had got a pint about dark. They argued and cussed over it—the others in the hollow could hear 'em—and he musta hit her purty hard a time or two.

"After they went to bed, he got up in the night and walked out in the yard to take a piss. She musta followed him out there and reached around and stabbed him right in the heart."

"She say anything?"

"No, sir. Just sulled up in the back seat and sat there. Got a big black eye and a bruise, bad bruise on her old arm."

"Be good if we can find the knife."

They stomped around through the weeds with their flashlights but found nothing. We went inside the rotting shack. There were some ramshackle chairs and a table. In the bedroom, a filthy mattress lay on the floor along with a reeking overflowing chamberpot. His overalls and a shirt hung on a nail, her clothing nowhere in sight.

"Probably the clothes on her back right now is all she owns."

"Yeah, they're living high on the hog, no doubt about it."

"Come back in the morning when it's daylight and look some more for the knife."

At the jail, the chief asked me if I could type. I said yes, I had learned at college. No, I wasn't as fast as a female typist, but I could get by, and my typing was easier to read than my writing done by hand. He smiled and said to get to work.

They had an old Underwood, heavy as an anvil, and we moved it out in the middle of the floor. I put two sheets of paper in it, with a carbon between them. Uncle Herman would get the carbon copy.

"What's yore name?" the chief asked the old woman. "And how old are you?"

She sat there on a low stool in the middle of the officers, with the doctor listening to the interrogation and the sound of my typewriter punctuating the conversation. She said her name was Sarah and she had a firm voice. Her eyes were defiant, her straggly hair flying this way and that as she jerked her head to face first the chief and then one of the night men.

"Where'd you get that black eye?" the night man asked.

"He give it to me. He was always beating on me."

"Is that why you killed him?"

She wouldn't answer when they accused her of his death, jerking her head and turning her gaze away. The chief tried it twice, got the same response both times.

"Who bought the pint of white likker?"

"I did."

"Where'd you get the money to buy the whiskey?"

"From cleaning up a house for a lady in town."

"Did you get to drink any of the likker?"

"No, he hit me and took it away from me. Never got to taste a drop."

"So that's why you killed him?"

"He hurt me all the time, beating on me. He never had no right to do that."

"So that's why you stabbed him."

She never gave an answer to a direct accusation, I noted on the typed report, and she was taken back to her cell after the chief made her sign my account of the questioning. She signed with a big X at the bottom, where I neatly typed her name. Of course, she couldn't read a word I had written, nor was she allowed to.

The chief of police read over my original, nodding his approval, and I openly folded up the carbon and put it in my pocket.

"Thanks for what you did. It looks good," he said. "Reckon we'll see her in court."

"You charging her?"

"Yeah, we'll try to find the knife later today and even if we don't, we'll charge her with murder. Let the grand jury have it." The cops took me back home and I slept like a log.

A FEW DAYS later, I headed back to the courthouse to see Darlene. Thoughts of her filled my head, but I had to remember that my visit had a purpose. The warrant, I had to remember the warrant.

"You still don't understand all about this, do you?" Uncle Herman asked. And he explained.

"The woman from Ramsey Hollow has had a hard life," he said, "and she infrequently works for your Aunt Hilda cleaning around and inside our house. Comes from good stock, but strong drink has ruined her for good. I hear from my sources that the police have charged her with murder."

"So you would defend her for free, since she works sometime at your house?"

"Not so fast, Wes, you have to be real careful with that word 'free.'"

"I should have known, counselor. It was my mistake."

He was smiling now, broadly, and nodding at his one pupil. Uncle Herman loved the spotlight and he liked it when I called him counselor or Your Honor. I always noticed speech patterns, and his conversations were obviously those of a lawyer—he was constantly dropping legal terms on me. Sometimes it was almost comical.

"This unfortunate woman will be standing before the bar of justice—"

"And not the bar at the country club."

"Nephew, you have interrupted me with a frivolous comment."

"My apology, sir, please continue."

"This poor defendant will be in dire need of competent counsel, which will probably be court-appointed."

"I'm beginning to see the light."

"This county, regardless of its rural nature, is rather liberal in its funding of legal assistance for defendants in capital cases."

"So you'll get some money from the system for defending her."

"I've got enough influence with the judge to get myself appointed in this case. I'll get a minimum fee and, of course, she will get a minimum performance from me. We'll end up pleading her on manslaughter and she'll get less than five years in women's prison. They'll feed her well there, too."

"Go visit the lovely Darlene," he said, "and get a good look at the warrant they served on our defendant inside the jail this morning."

"Tell me about Frog Cutshaw again."

"Mr. Cutshaw is a charming character. In addition to his regular activities, my sources tell me he's now getting into black-market tires."

"What? I heard he used to haul bootleg whiskey in boats and stuff, but I thought he just ran the store now."

"Well, the inside word is that the tires come by boat from Norfolk down to Wilmington and most of them are being sold there. But he's just got to be involved in selling a few here so they say he's put up a little garage behind his store and that's where they sell the tires."

"Him and his colored assistant?"

"Correct. The colored boy is loyal to him, probably out of fear, and nobody else knows the details."

"You said something about him going to see Darlene and why he was at the courthouse."

"Other women in the clerk's office tell me he tried to get Darlene to go out on a date with him more than once. But she'll have nothing to do with him, despite his persistence."

"But he's going to the courthouse for some other reason?" I didn't like even the thought of Frog with Darlene.

I had been persistent myself with her and it had paid off. The second time I asked her, she accepted and we went to the movie together in Carverville. After the movie, I had driven her to her parents' home there in town and walked her up on their front porch.

"My mama said you're supposed to show your appreciation when people have been nice to you," she told me in a low voice, and turned her pretty face up to be kissed.

Her lips had been sweet and warm but it was only for a moment and then she was gone. The memory was good.

"He's going to the courthouse," Uncle Herman said. "To politick with the county fathers on that Caney Fork road. He's got property out there which would be more valuable if there was a paved road to Caney Fork."

HIS COMMENTS echoed in my mind a week later when I headed out to Caney Fork on that familiar gravel road. Fifteen miles of roadway with two covered bridges—it would cost thousands of dollars to turn it into a paved road and the political bosses knew it.

Caney Fork Creek twists and turns like a blacksnake and the road follows the stream, staying to the lower ground and only crossing the creek where absolutely necessary since bridges are an expensive project.

The black-market tire buyers will create a little more traffic on the road, I thought to myself and had to grin at that. Frog could claim increased usage of his road, even if he caused it himself.

I had just crossed the covered bridge in the middle of the trip and started up a long straightaway when I realized that the crippled vet's house, where we had repaired the roof, was just on my right, and it was about a mile more to Cutshaw's Store.

Uncle Herman wanted me to check on a man who lived beyond the store, a fellow who was going to be involved in a lawsuit against the railroad. Wanted to know what kind of a house the man lived in, what kind of work he did. Uncle Herman, naturally, was being paid by the railroad.

"Take that new camera I bought you and take a picture of the man's house," he said. "You've got to learn to take good pictures. We may want you up in an airplane taking pictures. This is the twentieth century and we've got to modernize."

That was his latest thing—making pictures that could be shown to a jury to influence them. He had sent off for a professional camera like the newspapers used, not a Brownie box camera like most folks had. He said if I could learn to take good photos, he would hire a plane and I could take pictures of land along the planned highway and we could use them in court to sue for better prices for the landowners whose property was being taken.

So I had the new camera sitting on the seat beside me and I was sipping from the last of a fountain Coke I'd bought at the drugstore in Carverville where I bought film, when I came on the wreck.

"Who in hell sent for you?" Frog Cutshaw said. He was standing at the front of his big truck, which was resting on top of the smoking wreckage of what appeared to be an old car. "We don't need your ass here, Mr. Marine."

I ignored his snarling and walked around the scene, stooping to look at the mess under the truck. It was the crumpled Model-T of the crippled vet and the vet himself was still in it, apparently quite dead.

"My goddamn brakes failed on me—couldn't stop—that's what happened," Frog said loudly. "I don't see it's any o' your damn business, but that's the story." The colored youth who was his store clerk nodded agreement when Frog stared over at him.

"The Highway Patrol will want to come and look at this," I said.

"Well, by God, we're going back to the store. The bastards can come and look if they want to, but it's plain to see what happened and we're leaving."

"You're not supposed to leave where the accident happened."

"'You smart-talking turd, you just watch me. I'll leave right now."

An idea occurred to me—Uncle Herman would be proud. I brought out the shiny new camera and focused on the two vehicles still entangled. Another car had stopped now, two elderly women and a man walking up to the scene.

"What in God's hell are you doing?" Frog said, and his rage made his voice crack. "How come you taking pictures?"

"Just trying out my new camera."

"Well, try it out up your ass, you sonavabitch. You testify

against me and by God, you'll be sorry."

He jerked his big truck in gear and backed off the wreckage. The vehicle was loaded with sacks of fertilizer, probably weighed maybe ten times as much as the old flivver he'd just crushed. I noticed that the truck had a front bumper homemade from a five-foot section of railroad rail.

It's an old bootlegger's trick. I had heard of it but never actually seen it. Railroad rail weighs about ninety pounds per foot and having a bumper made from the stuff means about five hundred pounds of solid steel up front. If the police block the road on you, at seventy miles an hour, the vehicle becomes an unstoppable battering ram.

The crippled veteran never had a chance. With Frog's truck gone, I looked at his mangled body along with the other witnesses. The truck had shown no damage at all, but this old crate was almost unrecognizable as a car. The vet was already cold and stiff, blood dried on his face from the hot August sun.

"What's that laying alongside his leg?" the other driver said to me. "Looks like maybe a sword or something."

He helped me, and we got it free of the mess. It was a sword, still in its scabbard, with a cracked and dried leather belt and a tarnished brass buckle. The belt buckle was marked CSA.

"Well, I'll be doggoned," the witness said. "That's an old rebel sword from the war." He'd seen my camera and must've figured me for a minor official. "You better take the sword."

I did and drove to Uncle Jubal's to use the new phone there. Luckily, there was a highway patrolman at the sheriff's department when I reported the accident and I got to talk to him. In thirty minutes, we met at the scene, along with the ambulance from the local funeral home.

"Cutshaw, the other driver, he said his brakes failed?" the patrolman asked me.

"Yes sir, he did."

"And he was going to drive his big truck back to the store?"

"That's right."

"If his brakes are no good, how's he gonna stop the thing?"

"Good question, trooper. He didn't say."

"This is a long straight here. Looks like he would have seen this old T-model from a ways and had plenty of time to avoid hitting it."

I gave him my name, Uncle Herman's name, how to reach me. I saw no reason to tell him about my pictures or me having the sword. He said he was going on to the store to interview Frog Cutshaw and look at his truck. A small crowd had gathered to watch the funeral home men remove the body, and a wrecker was waiting to tow away what was left of the Model-T.

Six

"THIS IS THE third time we've gone to the movies," Darlene said.

"Are you bragging or complaining?"

"I'm not complaining," Darlene said, and gave me a look and a quick smile. She was sitting close to me as I drove us in Uncle Herman's coupe. "I'm having fun."

"Well, I'm glad you are. I am, too."

It was another hot August Saturday night in Carverville and the crowd at the theater reflected the times—a scarcity of young men. A few like me, wounded and sent home, but most either too young or too old for military service. But lots of girls giggled and looked at me.

"I'll have to keep an eye on you," Darlene said. "Your limp's not that bad. These girls would grab you in a minute."

I just laughed. I was content with what I had.

After the movie, we went to a hamburger place to eat and drink Cokes and talk.

"Do you drink?" she asked.

"I drink Cokes."

"No, I mean whiskey or beer."

"Naw, I drank a little beer in the Marines but I don't care much for it. It makes my legs wobbly and gives me a headache."

"Your uncle drinks. They say he has parties where people drink."

"Uncle Herman? Sure, he and my aunt are social drinkers."

"My people are Baptists and we're against liquor."

"Y'all are against dancing, too, aren't you?"

"Well, we're supposed to be."

"If I took you to a place where they had a band and dancing, would you dance with me?"

"Sure, I'd love to."

"That reminds me, did you hear the joke about the Baptists and dancing?"

"No, but I can tell that I'm going to hear it now."

"Do you know why Baptists never make love standing up?"

"No, tell me why."

"Because somebody might see them and think they were dancing."

"Ha-ha, very funny. Get me another Coke."

The thoughts of making love with sweet Darlene were on my mind now constantly but this would take careful planning. I brought two fresh Cokes back to our booth and we talked some more.

Then she allowed me to drive us to Hogan's Millpond, where we could talk and kiss a little. When the kissing got hot and heavy, she called it off and I took her home. And I got to kiss her good night. I loved her mouth.

"PUT ON A COAT and tie," Uncle Herman said. "You're not a lawyer, but you're my assistant and you need to look nice in court."

"I'm going to court today?"

"Yeah, Big Court is a real occasion. They found the knife."

"In Ramsey Hollow?"

"Well, they said they did. At least they're going to show us a knife . . ."

"Which means a real trial?"

"Probably not, but they'll threaten us."

"How's the woman taking it?"

"She doesn't know what's going on. She just trusts me to take care of her."

"They named you her lawyer."

"Certainly. That was done before his blood was even dry. I think, confidentially of course, that the police pulled this knife out of a drawer somewhere and are just saying that it was at the killing place."

"Fingerprints?"

"Naw, the knife they're showing is muddy and rusty and nasty. They never sent it to Raleigh for any kind of fingerprints. It'll just be their word that they found it behind that shack."

Big Court week was always an event in the county seat because it brought people to town. People normally came to town on Saturdays, but Big Court brought folks in who were on jury duty, who had relatives to be tried, or who were spectators at the best free show in the county.

Small-town merchants took advantage of the increased traffic and dragged out their dusty SALE signs and thereby increased their own take. Two of the cafés put signs out on the sidewalk advertising their blue plate specials. It was very festive.

"You wanna see the chief?" the desk officer in Carverville's small police station asked.

"Yeah, just for a minute. I know he's a busy man today."

The desk officer grinned at me and shook his head, tugging at my tie, sticking his tongue out and doing a mimicry of choking.

"Are you preaching somewhere today? You look funny wearing that tie."

"Uncle Herman made me."

The chief heard us and motioned for me to come back into his tiny, glass-walled office. A trusty from the nearby county jail was wiping down the windows. The prisoner was young, black and wore prison striped pants and a short-sleeved shirt.

"Don't pay no mind to this boy," the chief said. "He's bad to fight, doing sixty days, so the sheriff lets me have him once in a while as a janitor."

"Can I see the knife?"

"Yeah, I reckon."

"We'll see it soon enough in court, but Herman wanted me to at least take a look at it."

He reached into a desk drawer and carefully brought out the weapon and placed it on the worn wood surface between us. It was a rusty old paring knife, with a wooden handle and a small, thin blade. There had been mud on it, most of it wiped away, but it still felt dirty and smelled like damp earth. It had obviously been buried.

"We found it under the front porch of their shack," he said, forcing a serious manner he could assume on the witness stand. "There is a stain on the handle that we think is blood."

I could tell that he was lying and that he didn't want to be questioned about it. But I made an effort anyway. "Chief, I was there that night. The man bled out in three heartbeats. This blade looks too short to do the business . . ."

"I've said all I'm gonna say 'til they put me on the stand." He leaned over the desk now, looking me right in the face. "I like your uncle, I need his support and, hell, everybody knows I want to be sheriff sometime. We'll try to help y'all all we can. We appreciate you typing up our report that night. But the district attorney is on my ass . . ."

The room got quiet then, except for the squeaking sound of the trusty's rag on the window glass. The chief had said all he wanted to, and I couldn't think of anything to say. Then he forced a little smile at me and broke the tension.

"Come 'ere boy," he said with amusement to the trusty. "I want you to show Junior your arm."

Obediently, the trusty put down his pail and rag and stood at the end of the chief's desk. Slowly, he extended his left arm palm down for inspection. There were several raised scars on his forearm's upper surface, between wrist and elbow, the scars having a segmented appearance where catgut stitches had pulled the flesh together.

"Our town doctor," the chief said. "Don't like drinking and fighting. I swear, I think he does that to punish 'em, black or white. Don't matter who it is, if they've been cut in a knife fight, he pulls his stitches way too tight and it makes the ugliest scars you ever saw.

"All these young bucks that like to fight end up taking the other man's blade on the arm, where they've throwed up their left hand and they've got their own knife in their right. Them scars are terrible. Show 'im y'r neck, bo."

Meekly, the trusty thrust his head forward and pulled back

at his collar, allowing a look at the back of his head and neck. There was a raised, ribbed scar about two inches long at the collar-line, an obscene pink and black thing that looked like a caterpillar.

"He almost got you with that one, didn't he?" the chief said. "If that cut had been a little deeper, mighta sent you to the graveyard."

I went back to the law office educated on local knife-fighting and convinced that the police were framing my aunt's cleaning woman.

"THE DISTRICT attorney is a sonuvabitch," Uncle Herman said, lighting his black Cuban cigar with a flaring wooden kitchen match.

"Herman, don't use coarse language. It sounds so common . . ." Aunt Hilda said.

"It's true," Uncle Herman insisted.

The quick sulphur smell of the match faded away, replaced by the pungent odor of his cigar as Uncle Herman commented on courthouse characters. We sat on the porch after dinner, night falling on the residential street, Herman in his favorite Brumby rocker from Atlanta, Aunt Hilda and me in a creaky porch swing.

"Did you see the sheriff's hair today?"

"Yes, honey, I saw it."

"Honestly, it's hilarious."

"Well, Hilda, for God's sake, it is an election year."

"I know but it's so obvious . . ."

"He dyes his hair every time we have Big Court, you know that."

I was grinning in the darkness and he knew it, playing to me now. "Wes, did you see him, too?"

The sheriff's hair had turned gray, but for court week, he usually had it colored back toward its original red. The dye job was a terrible fake champagne-pink color, but the sheriff never realized that. He just plowed into crowds shaking hands and hugging babies like he was Roosevelt.

"The country folks say the comb on the old rooster gets bright-red sometimes," Herman said, chuckling as he flicked cigar ashes over the railing into the camellia bush.

"Don't burn my bushes down," she said, adding, "and I don't think that remark about the rooster has anything to do with getting votes. Maybe about making baby chicks."

"I was just saying that our sheriff has always been a moral man," he said. "Very different from our district attorney, who is a weasel."

Even though they couldn't see me in the warm darkness, I had to nod on that one. The district attorney was small and dark for a white man, with quick movements and a sharp nose. Very appropriate description.

"That's pretty good," I said. I had been listening, but it was the first time I had spoken that evening. Mostly, I just listened to them. "When I was in the ninth grade over here at the high school, one of the boys brought a weasel to class."

"What did it look like? I've never seen one," Aunt Hilda said.

"Well, it was in a clear gallon-sized jar with a wide-mouth lid on it. I remember the teacher made us all gather around and look at it. It reminded me of a snake with fur and little legs. Its body really was long and snaky. And it had bright beady eyes, like the district attorney . . ."

"He's dark, too, Herman. I think he's a Jew," Aunt Hilda said.

"No, dear, Jew lawyers stay in the big cities. You wouldn't find one prosecuting bootleggers out here in the backwoods."

"That reminds me, Herman, I saw downtown today that Harry Richter's got his shirts on sale this week. You need to get some new shirts."

"Hilda, my dear," he said, sighing with patience. "Our conversation about Jews caused you to think about shirts on sale?"

Apparently, she was getting tired of ironing the frayed collars and ragged cuffs on several of his.

"You see what you'll have to face some day, Wes. My wife and her colored girl are ganging up on me, making me buy more shirts. A man has to get used to being bossed by women, get used to petticoat rule. Anyway, I don't think Richter is a Jew, I think he's actually Lebanese."

"You know what I mean, Herman. Stop in there tomorrow and buy some shirts. If the family is dark-skinned and they sell shoes and clothing in a small town in the South, they're Jews as far as I'm concerned."

"Hilda can be very opinionated, Wes, I'm warning you."

"Don't you worry about Wes. You're not the only one that's educating him. I've sent him down to the library and got him reading some good books. Have you finished that Faulkner book, yet, son?"

"Yes ma'am," I said, "and I don't understand a lot of it."

Uncle Herman said Faulkner was too liberal about race, and added that Hilda was too.

"Well, this country is changing," she said. "Wes, you listen to me. I've already given up on Herman. If you're going to be a lawyer sometime in the future, you need to understand things and how they all fit together. There's a lot more to the world than Carverville."

"He knows that, Hilda. Lord, he's been out in the Pacific, to Hawaii, California, lots of places . . ."

"I know that, but I'm talking about the social part of it, the politics and all. Don't pay any attention to him, Wes, just listen to me. The big farmers, the plantation people, that's what started this country. Virginia people like Washington and Jefferson, they all had big farms and slaves and while their farms about ran themselves, they read books and talked about the issues and set up this nation to suit themselves."

"She's from the Piedmont, Wes, remember that. She's a linthead." Uncle Herman was kidding her, I knew that, especially when he reached over and patted her arm. His cigar was now just a red dot in the darkness.

"My folks were cotton mill workers, but I never worked in the mill, so don't dare call me a linthead. But it's a good point.

Up in the middle part of North Carolina, where I was raised, there has always been some industry. Every little town had a cotton mill, taking in bales of cotton and shipping out thread. Folks worked so many hours a week and got paid a wage. It's not farming like Eastern North Carolina. It's industry and that means money and lots of merchants, lots of stores for people to spend their money.

"Down here, it's still mostly farming. The boll weevil has about ruined cotton farming so they're turning more and more to tobacco. Slavery's gone, but we still have lots of blacks here, more than the Piedmont."

"He was raised here," Uncle Herman said. "He already knows about his own home county."

But she pressed on, saying, "He spent his younger days logging out in the swamps or in a classroom. He needs the big picture.

"So the big old-time planters are gone," she said. "Now you have some smaller farmers but also a lot of small businessmen who have taken over the political power. They are the ones that run things and they're going to have to move toward industry. People need jobs."

She said there were hundreds of textile mills and furniture plants in the middle part of the state and that the East was going to have to get industry. Tractors were replacing plow mules and hordes of blacks weren't going to be needed on the farms.

"Where are they going to go?" I asked.

"Lots of them are going North, Wes. Going right now to get jobs in Washington and Baltimore and New York City. There's jobs for 'em there and not as much prejudice against them. I don't blame them a bit. My house girl talks about it all the time."

"You ought to be in politics, Hilda," Uncle Herman said. "My cigar's gone out and it's getting close to bedtime. I'm going inside."

"Wait a minute, what about your defendant tomorrow? And the SOB you mentioned to us earlier?" I asked him.

"They've got an old knife to throw on the table," Uncle

Herman said. "We'll have to argue in chambers, a private affair, Wes, that you'll be in on and you'll probably enjoy. She killed him, but probably not with that knife. We'll end up pleading her for the least prison time we can get."

THE NEXT DAY in court was a real lesson in lawyering, not out in the old high-ceilinged, pine-paneled courtroom, but behind closed doors in the judge's chambers.

Uncle Herman and the district attorney had made sniping remarks at each other all morning and the old judge was getting tired of it.

"Gentlemen, I'm tired of these theatrics. I want to see both of you in chambers."

"He has hemorrhoids," Uncle Herman whispered. "By this time, late in the week, he's ready to call it quits and go on to his next town, the next session down the road. If we press for a full trial, he'll have to stay here next week. The DA's ready for a week of it, but not this judge."

He and I followed the DA and his two assistants back behind the jury room, down a cool hallway, to the office reserved for the visiting judge. We left the defendant sitting alone at our table with about fifty spectators, at least ten of them relatives of the dead husband.

"Let's get this settled, boys," the judge said. He poured a water glass half-full of amber whiskey from a bottle hidden in the desk, took a swig and sat back in his civilian clothes to listen to the debate. "That damn robe is getting hot."

"This man was murdered, plain and simple, by his wife," the district attorney said, glaring at Uncle Herman. "I won't take a plea for anything less than second-degree. We've got a weapon and we've got witnesses."

I could tell he took it personally. He believed he was the will of the people, some sort of avenging angel who would set things right.

"You've got nothing," Uncle Herman said, quietly but with conviction. He could orate like a Bible-thumping evangelist in the courtroom, but here, there was no need. "You've got absolutely nothing. Your witnesses are a bunch of sorry drunks, whose brains have been muddled by alcohol, and your so-called knife is a fraud."

"Sir, I resent your remarks—"

"You hush 'til I get through. You're in my town now, and I'm gonna tell you straight. That knife is a hoax—it's got a blade way too small to have done the damage that man suffered. You put pressure on the police to find a knife and they got you one, but you're framing this poor woman."

"Judge, I don't think we're getting anywhere with this and I'm ready to go to full trial on behalf of the deceased," the DA said.

"Hold on," the judge said, sipping thoughtfully on his whiskey. "There's no need for a trial in this matter. Herman, how much prison time will you accept? And did this woman work in your household? Come clean now. Somebody told me she did."

"Yeah, she works occasionally for my wife."

The DA looked at me now—he wouldn't look at Herman—and muttered something to his assistant.

"We'll take a plea on second-degree murder and recommend ten years," the DA said. He really did look like a weasel, his sharp-pointed nose jerking this way and that, his eyes beady and piercing. "The dead man's brothers want significant punishment for the woman."

"People in hell want a drink of ice water," Uncle Herman said, plainly enjoying this verbal battle. "But they don't get it. When your coroner takes the stand, I'm gonna ask him in his professional opinion if he thinks your little peeling knife made the wound he saw in that man's heart. When he answers, your case is gonna fall apart in your lap."

The DA's dark face took on a pained expression, like someone had suddenly kicked him in the crotch. He turned to look at the judge, who was draining the last of his drink.

"Herman, what do you want?" the judge said.

The pecking order had been established. I think that's what

they call it. Uncle Herman and the judge would work things out, the DA was merely an advisor. Righteous indignation on Herman's part at the faked evidence had sealed the deal, but the relationship between my uncle and the visiting judge had set the stage.

"We'll plead to manslaughter," Uncle Herman said, and the DA's assistants took down every word he uttered. "We want a sentence of five years, with only one year to be active prison time at the women's prison in Raleigh, the remaining four years to be probation here in Carverville. Supervised, of course, by the state probation officers."

There was a long silence and the DA stared a hole in me, as if I had a prime part in this. He still wouldn't look at Uncle Herman.

"What do you say, Mr. District Attorney?" the judge asked.

The DA looked at the notes his assistant had written on a yellow legal pad and then looked up at the ceiling fan, turning slowly in the late August heat. Finally, he looked only at the judge, and nodded. "Yeah, we'll take that."

The judge motioned for the DA and his men to leave the room, and for Uncle Herman and me to stay. When the door closed behind them, he grinned and reached for his robe. I helped him into the robe—it seemed like the right thing to do.

"Herman, it's always a pleasure to do business in your courthouse. You did well just now, but if you'd pushed harder, you might have got her off completely. Why did you agree to a year of prison?"

"Well, for several reasons. First of all, I believe she did really kill her husband. Probably with a butcher knife, which they never found. But he beat her up all the time and they both drank heavily and she finally got the nerve to put the blade to him."

"Some of them say to 'stob' him?"

"Yeah, Wes here went out there that night and he'd sure been stabbed. So she needs a little punishment, but just a little. They'll feed her well in prison and she's got some bad teeth—the state will take care of her dental work while she's in Raleigh."

"I see," the judge said, chuckling as we walked down the

hallway back to court. "And you were probably afraid you or your wife would be paying for the dental work if she stayed here."

"Could be, something like that. And before I forget it, Herman, thanks for the whiskey. Your pink-haired sheriff tried to give me a gallon of moonshine likker. Imagine that? White likker. I can't drink that stuff. He ought to know that."

A WEEK OR SO after Labor Day, the trooper who was investigating the fatal crash came to see me at the law office.

"I need to complete my report," he said. "If you don't mind, I need you to look over what I've got here and sign at the bottom saying you approve or agree with how I've stated what you said."

His report was simple and straightforward, quoting me as the witness who arrived first on the scene. It showed diagrams of the doomed Model-T and Frog Cutshaw's big truck, and listed the driver's names. The cause of the crash was listed as "failure of brake on truck."

"What did you find that day at the store?" I asked.

"He said the truck was parked behind the store and there was a puddle of brake fluid under the vehicle, beside the bottom of the right front tire."

"Did you get a look at that railroad rail for a front bumper?" I asked.

"Yes sir, I did. Anything gets hit with that will be in a world of hurt," he said. "It's heavy-duty for sure."

"Will you be charging Cutshaw with any crime?"

"I don't think so," the trooper said. "But I'm leaving it up to the DA. It's his job and he'll have my report and your name. If it goes any farther than this, it's up to him."

I still didn't tell him about the photographs I'd made that day. Herman said there was no need to tell everything and we had a right to take photographs anywhere we wanted to.

"The pictures might be useful if Mr. Cutshaw is prosecuted," Uncle Herman said, "and they may be very useful if we sue Cutshaw on behalf of the dead man's widow. You need to go see her very soon and discreetly offer her our services in this matter. Maybe show her the pictures, if she can stand to look at them."

"One other thing," the trooper said as he stood to leave. "Inside the wreckage of that old car, tucked under the seat, we found two live hand grenades. Had to call the military police to come and take them away from here. Know anything about that?"

I shook my head and he left.

Uncle Herman's secretary came and said I had a telephone call from Uncle Jubal. That was strange. Uncle Jubal had a telephone out at Caney Fork but he had never once called me in town. He wasn't comfortable with the phone and, besides, with the party line setup, he knew any conversation was likely to be heard by the neighborhood gossips who listened in on all calls.

"We haven't got to see you in a while, Wes," he said. His voice was oddly formal and he seemed agitated but I couldn't figure it out.

"Your aunt's gonna kill a chicken tomorrow and we've got some good beans and corn out of the garden. We want you to drive out here and eat supper with us tomorrow night." He paused and I almost responded, but he began speaking again, rushing to get the words out. "And we want you to spend the night with us."

I needed to go to Caney Fork anyway to see the vet's widow so it would work out fine, I thought, but the expressed desire for me to spend the night wasn't normal. And the invitation would likely have come from Aunt Alma, not him. I accepted and he hung up.

"I was thinking about our little game with the DA the other day," Uncle Herman said later. He was leaning back in his big chair and clasping his hands over his belly. "That DA is a true-enough SOB, just like I said out on the porch that night, isn't he?"

"Yes sir, he is that for sure."

I pondered for a moment on the vicious nature of the DA

and then told him most of my recent conversations with the trooper and Uncle Jubal. I didn't tell him every detail—no use to bother him with trivial stuff if it wasn't needed. I wanted to keep the dead vet's Confederate sword if I could, for a souvenir.

I would talk earnestly with his widow tomorrow, making a polite request for Uncle Herman to represent her in a lawsuit against Frog Cutshaw for wrongful death of her husband. I would show her the photos I had and speak with emotion of how I had found the scene and her husband.

But why had her husband been driving his rickety old car toward Frog Cutshaw's store, armed with an old Rebel sword and two grenades?

Seven

"SO WHEN ARE we going to a place to dance?" Darlene asked.

"I wish you'd listen. This good Baptist girl and she's talking about dancing."

"You said you'd take me to a place to dance."

"I'll take you to Roy's Rhythm Ranch."

"Ha-ha, very funny. I'm not going to that old place."

"Just because they sell white likker out there and have a few fights once in awhile, you'd turn up your pretty nose . . . ?"

"I've heard too much about that place."

Aunt Hilda prodded me constantly to know when they were going to meet my girlfriend. She and Uncle Herman were members of the country club and there was a dance there for members coming up in a week or two. They had a swing band coming in from Norfolk, guys who played horns and violins and wore suits, not the rank hillbilly musicians that made the rafters ring out at the Rhythm Ranch.

"Well, they're having a dance out at the country club in about two weeks."

"I'd love to go," she said, and her smile said it all. I loved the way her eyes looked when she was happy. "I've already heard about it. But it's for members only."

"We can go as guests of Uncle Herman. It's not a problem."

She was so happy she leaned across the front counter of the Clerk of Court's office and gave me a little peck on the cheek. I caught the quick scent of her and her warm lips on my face made me a little dizzy. Then she just as quickly went back to being all business.

"They took your client to prison this morning, a deputy sheriff driving her all the way to Raleigh to the women's prison.

They had to have a woman with him in the car so one of the women from our office went, too.

"And she's been telling everybody in the jail that your Uncle Herman is going to get her teeth fixed," Darlene went on, laughing now. "Is that really true?"

"That's what he says," I told her. "He'll send a letter to the corrections department in a week or two and get things going. He knows everybody and the state senator from this district is a close friend of his. Which will also be mentioned in the letter, I'm sure."

"What am I going to wear to the dance? Let's talk about something that's really important."

"I don't care. Men don't know anything about that stuff."

"Ask your aunt. She goes to things at the country club. She'll know. I haven't met her; can't ask her."

"Sure, I'll ask for you," I said. And I thought to myself that I really ought to arrange a quiet Saturday night dinner at the country club for Darlene to meet them, just two couples getting together. Then I told her that I had to leave. I was going out to Caney Fork to meet a young woman.

"What?"

"You heard me. I've got to go talk to a young woman out at Caney Fork."

"Wesley Ross, you better not be running around on me."

"Just kidding, honey. It's business, that's all."

"It better be." And her hand made an advance across the counter to gently hold mine.

I was well aware of the soft, moist warmth of it. Lowering my voice, I told her of the vet's wife and the purpose of my planned visit. And I told her I would be eating supper with Uncle Jubal and Aunt Alma, and spending the night there.

"They must have got lonesome for you."

"I suppose." Still, it was a strange invitation and something about it puzzled me. "I've got to go."

"Drive carefully," she said, and pulled me toward her for a good-bye kiss.

I got dizzy again, and it was painful to leave.

I GOT TO THE dead man's place about three that afternoon. Some folks keep old junk cars, even wrecks, in their yards for parts, but I suppose since there was a death involved, she wouldn't want to see it around. Their yard was grown up in weeds; at first glance you would have thought nobody lived there.

But the front door was open and there was a smell of meat cooking on the woodstove. I always felt sorry for womenfolk who had to cook, black or white, over a woodstove in late August. No wonder women prodded their husbands to buy the newfangled electric stoves if they could afford it, and if they were in a place that had electricity.

And this house had electric power. I could see the overhead wires. There was a main line that came up from Carverville that fed most of Caney Fork, but she was sure cooking on wood.

"Anybody home?" I shouted real loud, knocking on the rough wood door frame and peering into the house through the screen door. "Anybody here?"

"I'm sorry, I didn't hear you drive up," she said, wiping her hands on her apron as she came to the door. "Please come in."

"I'm Wesley Ross."

"I know who you are. I remember you being here to help get the house fixed up for us. It was good of the church men to help us. We appreciated it."

Her voice was low, almost a whisper. I could barely hear her. She looked at me once, then dropped her eyes and now looked away from me as she talked.

"Can we sit down somewhere?" I asked.

She didn't speak but led me to the kitchen table, an old unpainted wooden piece without even a cloth on it. It had seen years of use, obviously a hand-me-down from relatives, and its surface was stained dark and had a greasy sheen. I put a manila envelope on the table that held the wreck photographs, but I wouldn't show them unless she agreed to look at them. "I'm sorry about your husband getting killed in the wreck."

She smiled and nodded, but didn't reply and looked out the window. In profile, her face looked thin and drawn, her eyes red and bleary, maybe from crying.

"Ma'am, I work for my uncle. He's a lawyer at Carverville and if you might need a lawyer, he's an awful good one. Your man has been taken away from you and you may want to sue Frog Cutshaw for causing his death."

She looked right at me then, her mouth open in amazement and then something like fear seemed to set in. Her hands fluttered at her throat first and then her apron and she shook her head. "No, I couldn't do that," she said, her voice timid and low. "They never even charged him with nothing."

"We know that, but a civil case can still be made against him. You could get money or maybe even land out of him."

"What's in that envelope?"

"I was the first one to arrive at the wreck that day and I took pictures for my uncle to use in court. I've got pictures, if you want to look at them."

"Does it show him . . . my husband?"

"Yeah, a couple of them show the body before it was removed."

"Well, I don't need to see them. I'll take your word for it."

"I'm sorry, ma'am. I can hardly hear you."

"I don't want to see the pictures. I'll take your word for it that they're okay."

"All right. Now you think about what I told you and I'm writing down this telephone number for you. It's my uncle's law office in Carverville."

"We ain't got no phone."

"That's all right. You could go somewhere and call him, or you can come to this office. He'll want to talk with you before we take any action on this."

She pinched her lips together, looked down at the floor and shook her head again. Then I told her about the old rebel sword I took from the wreckage.

"You can have it to keep," she said. "I'm tired of looking at the old thing; it used to hang over the door."

"Well, thank you. I might hang it over my door."

"I'm keeping the new rifle he brought home from the war,

but I'm getting rid of everything else. Thanks for coming out."

We shook hands and I drove toward supper at Uncle Jubal's place.

AFTER SUPPER, Uncle Jubal took his Bible down from the mantel and told me to follow him upstairs. I was more than puzzled.

"Send the others up when they get here," was all he said to Aunt Alma.

He and I went into an upstairs bedroom where we could still feel the heat of the day. Windows were open and there was a promise of cooler evening air coming through the window screens. The room was lit by a single bare electric bulb, hanging from the center of the ceiling on a twisted two-strand cord. There was a table with a basin and empty water pitcher beside the bed, for the convenience of guests. Uncle Jubal wearily put the pitcher and basin under the bed and moved the table to the center of the room along with the room's only chair.

"What are we doing, Uncle Jubal?"

"You'll see soon enough, Wes, just be patient. I've plowed all day and I'm wore out."

He seated himself in the chair, placed his Bible on the table and I sat down on the bed. We could hear heavy footsteps coming up the stairs.

"Good evening, boys, thanks for coming."

"Howdy, Jubal ... hot enough for you?" one of them asked.

Dressed in bib overalls and work-boots, Uncle Jubal's three brothers entered the room. They were shy country men who farmed adjacent land, all younger than Jubal. Despite his short leg and his limp, Jubal walked among them as a leader. Everyone shook hands with him.

"I don't have a son," Jubal said, "so I've got Wes with me tonight. We may need some young men in this before it's over, but I hope not. Y'all can sit on the floor or the bed or stand—we don't have enough chairs for everybody. Wes, pull the shades down if you don't mind."

There were no curtains in this room, but there were cheap cotton shades and I pulled them down, which would keep the proceedings private but also would keep out any cooling breeze. Jubal sat down at his impromptu pulpit and the farmers stood. I sat on the bed.

"Something awful has happened. I don't hardly know how to start telling it," Uncle Jubal said. "But before I start, I think we ought to go to the Lord in prayer."

They took off their hats and stood obediently in front of his reading table, almost like he was a judge or something. Jubal was a longtime deacon in their church and they were used to him praying at every occasion. I bowed my head, too, but it was strange.

Uncle Jubal prayed a short prayer, thanked the Lord for the good rain we'd been getting and the crops nearly done. And he asked for strength and wisdom for all of us in the struggle that we would soon be facing, and that we would do his will. I wondered about that last sentence.

"I want to read y'all two passages of scripture," he said. "It'll help you understand what we've got to do here and will show you what is right. And I may have to preach to you a little, too."

They stood patiently, listening to their older brother, and he thumbed through his old Bible, the cover worn slick from handling and carrying to church every Sunday for the past forty years. Then he found his first reference.

"Listen to this; hear the word from the Book. This is the Law.

"Leviticus twenty-four, verses twenty to twenty-one: 'Breach for breach, eye for eye, tooth for tooth: as he hath caused a blemish in a man, so shall it be done to him again. And he that killeth a beast, he shall restore it: and he that killeth a man, he shall be put to death.'"

He read that to us quietly, letting it sink in, three times. We looked at each other but nobody said anything.

Uncle Jubal grimaced, turned to another place in his old

Bible and read another to us.

"Deuteronomy twenty-one, verses twenty-two to twenty-three: 'And if a man have committed a sin worthy of death, and he be put to death, and thou hang him on a tree: His body shall not remain all night upon the tree, but thou shalt in any wise bury him that day; (for he that is hanged is accursed of God;) that thy land be not defiled, which the Lord thy God giveth thee for an inheritance.'"

He read that one to us twice, his voice low and slow, letting the words burn into our ears.

"Don't you see, boys. The old-timey Jews had to execute people from time to time. Especially for murder, for killing innocent people."

We looked at him then, not understanding.

"Boys, what I'm trying to tell you is this. We're gonna have to kill Frog Cutshaw."

You could have heard a pin drop. Really, I mean it. The brothers looked at each other and I looked down at the bare floor. Uncle Jubal shifted position and his chair creaked.

"We appreciate the Bible, brother," the youngest farmer said, and smiled just a little. There was a mischief in his eyes, even with the family shyness. "But I shore hope you don't want to hang ol' Frog. He's so fat we'll never find a rope strong enough to hold him."

We all grinned then, no laughter, but it broke the tension in the room. Uncle Jubal leaned back in his chair, looked right at each one of us. "He's a sorry excuse for a man," Jubal said, and began to tell us the story. The youngest brother now sat on the bed with me, the others remained standing. "That Army boy we fixed up the house for? You remember him. He got killed in the wreck with Frog's truck? Well, here's the whole truth.

"You remember he's all wounded, moving into that old house with his young wife. What's her name, June? And she is young and purty and some of our younger men were looking at her that day. You remember, don't you Wes?

"Well, it wasn't too long after that she walked to the store by herself. It's about a mile, and they usually drove his old

T-model. But she said he was gone somewhere that day, so she walked by herself. She kept all this to herself, wouldn't tell nobody, but she finally broke down a day or two ago and told my wife when we took some garden vegetables over there to her. It'll make you furious mad to hear it.

"June said she went into Frog's store alone and there wasn't nobody there but Frog and that young colored man that helps him."

"That one you're talking about is a brother to the colored woman that lives here on your place, ain't it Jubal?" the youngest brother asked from the bed beside me.

"Yeah, Ruby and her children are all the tenants I've got now," Jubal said. "Her man left her back in the spring and I can't find nobody to take his place. Her brother, the one over at the store, his name is Reuben, but he don't like farm work. I talked to him, but he won't budge."

"Get back to the story."

"Well, anyway, June told my wife that she was in the store by herself and Frog come out from behind the counter and put his arm around her. Before she knew what was happening, he had that colored boy to lock the front door and he tore June's clothes off and raped her right there, standing up in the middle of the store."

Silence again, heads shaking.

"She told my wife that he got her from behind, rode her like a big boar hog, both of them buck naked right there in the store. Said she cried and begged him not to do it, but he done it anyway. Hurt her inside, too, she said."

"I reckon he musta thought he was Big Boy hisself," the youngest brother said. "Frog's real proud o' that big stud-boar he's got. Claims ol' Big Boy can ride them sows down if they ain't strong. His weight is so much he breaks their hindquarters sometimes."

"Well, he ain't got no right to breed another man's wife," one of the other brothers said. "That's rape, plain and simple. And they was naked and the nigger seen her?"

Uncle Jubal nodded solemnly. I knew he didn't like to hear

the term *nigger* in his house, but he let it pass this time. "And that's not all," he said.

"June told my wife she got her clothes back on, could hardly walk, trembling and crying, and they unlocked the door and let her out. She walked home, cleaned herself up and wouldn't tell her husband for a day or two. But he knew something was wrong and she finally told him. He said, according to June, that Frog was going to die and that a man that bad didn't deserve to die quickly from a gun. He had an old Confederate sword from his family and that's what he took with him on his last ride. Said he was gonna cut Frog to pieces, cut off his pecker first and then his head with that terrible sword."

I didn't say anything about the grenades but I couldn't help thinking about them. If the Army vet had tossed two grenades into the store first, there wouldn't have been much left of Frog to hack up with the sword. Good plan.

"I'd say that the Army boy headed out for the store to kill Frog just as Frog and the colored man come down the road in that big truck loaded with fertilizer. Frog recognized what was happening and just flat run over that boy and killed him."

"That was probably the oldest T-model Ford still on the road around here," one of the brothers said. "I don't see how he kept it a-running."

"It was helt together with wire. It shook all over when it did run," another said.

"Well, it sure did shake I bet when Frog hit it with the truck," Uncle Jubal said firmly. It was hard to hold this crowd on the subject. "I'm saying that this man deserves to die. He raped June and run over her husband. We can't expect any justice from the courthouse. Frog's kin to the sheriff and we'll have to do it ourselves."

They nodded and I watched.

"Frog would have shot that boy dead with his pistol if he'd come at Frog at the store," the youngest said. I still didn't mention the grenades, didn't see any reason to. "He's fast as lightning with that .45 automatic, even for a fat man. We'll have to keep that in mind."

"Jubal, what do you want to do? How will we do it?" one of the brothers said.

Uncle Jubal said he'd given it much thought. It was our duty to kill Frog Cutshaw, he said, but we didn't want to be caught for it, much less on trial at the courthouse. We would be sneaky, he said, and ambush Frog at his hog lot, where the prized Big Boy and the other hogs were fed each morning.

"Now, Jubal, he don't come down there every morning his own self. He sends that boy Reuben a lot of the time."

The big hog lot was located across the road from the store, but probably a half-mile from it, on low ground along Caney Fork Creek. A dirt road led down to the hog lot from the store. The creek was the boundary between Uncle Jubal's farm and Frog's property, the land around the hog lot heavily wooded, and on Uncle Jubal's side of the stream lay a large cornfield.

"There ain't no foot log across the creek, is there Jubal?"

"No," Uncle Jubal answered, "we've never been good neighbors and there never was the usual foot log. I can hear his hogs squealing easy from that field every time I'm down there. Now stop talking and listen to me.

"He treasures them hogs, especially Big Boy, and this is how we'll bushwhack him," Uncle Jubal said. "Working at night so nobody'll see us, we'll put in a temporary foot log to cross the creek from my field to his land. And we'll kill one of his little pigs and cut its head off. We'll put that pig's head on his doorstep at the store that very night. The next morning when Frog and the colored man open the store, they'll see that pig's head lying there and ol' Frog will roar and rage and come a-flying down to the hog lot. And that's when one of us'll shoot him, when he steps out of the truck."

"What are we gonna shoot him with?"

"I've thought about that some and I've listened to Wes tell about his gun in the big fight agin the Japs last year. I think we need to buy a shotgun, a repeater that will shoot three or four times to make sure he's dead."

"Sounds good. None of us got anything like that; we just got single-shooters."

"Single-barrel shotgun is all we ever need for rabbit hunting."

"Well, we ain't rabbit hunting now. This is serious business."

"Raped a married woman and run plumb over her husband."

"I never believed that story about his brakes failing anyhow."

"We'll send two of our wives out to Wilmington," Uncle Jubal said. "They can buy a 12 gauge repeater and some buckshot out there, bring it back here and nobody'll know."

"Who's gonna do the shooting? Wes could probably do it good."

"This is a Caney Fork problem and Wes ain't gonna do the shooting," Uncle Jubal said. "Us four brothers are gonna draw straws to see who does it."

"You right sure you don't want to roll dice or cut a deck of cards?" the youngest brother said grinning, kidding Jubal about his strict Baptist attitudes.

"You're trying to make a joke, brother," Jubal said. "It ain't time for joking. We've got an evil beast living amongst us."

"I know, I know, din't mean nothing by it."

The serious tone of the proceedings now re-established, Uncle Jubal reached into his shirt pocket and drew out a small group of broom straws. "Give me your hat," he said to the nearest brother, and set the hat on the table in front of him, the sweat-stained inner band and the battered brim facing upward.

"I'm gonna put four straws into this hat. See here, four straws I got from Alma's broom downstairs. Three of 'em are white, one is red, see? With four straws inside the hat, Wes is gonna hold up the hat about face level so nobody can see down inside it and we're gonna draw.

"The man that gets the red straw will do the actual shooting. Everybody else will help with putting in the foot log, killing the decoy hog, anything else. Even putting in twenty dollars apiece to buy the gun with, okay?"

They nodded approval and gathered in close to the table.

Jubal showed us the four straws—three white and one red—and dumped them into the hat. I picked up the hat by the brim, holding it level about head-high, and shook it good.

One by one, they reached into the hat, felt around and drew out a straw.

Uncle Jubal drew last and pulled out slowly, staring intently at his own hand, clasping a broom straw the color of blood.

Eight

"YOU LOOK NICE in your new suit," Darlene said.

I grinned. "Thank you, and you always look good to me."

"I thought we came here to dance. "

"Listen to the Baptist girl, suggesting a dance."

"I might as well suggest it. Looks like you're not going to do anything unless I suggest it."

"Well, in that case, let's dance."

"I thought you'd never ask."

Uncle Herman and Aunt Hilda sat at the same table with us at the country club ballroom and were obviously amused by our conversation. They'd heard every word and laughed at the way Darlene and I talked to each other.

Sweet Darlene smelled so good and was so soft in my arms as we danced to the smooth music of the orchestra. With my limp, I knew I was awkward but she wanted to try it.

This way, she'd say, and move me into the proper positions, turning us and guiding us through the waltz patterns. I was a willing student but clumsy.

Other couples whirled and glided with ease around us, mostly middle-aged and older folks. I saw one soldier in uniform there with his girl, obviously on furlough from the war. It was a tame, genteel affair compared to the roadhouse chaos I had observed before the war at Roy's Rhythm Ranch.

"Did you really go out to that honky-tonk place?" she asked back at the table when we sat down to rest. "That bad Roy's place we heard about?"

"Yeah, the last year I was home before I went in the Marines, I went out there with some friends a time or two. Rough place."

"Tell me about it. I'd never go to a place like that."

"Well they had a hillbilly band, all guitars and fiddles and banjo music, nothing like this dance orchestra music. They played real loud and fast and the dancing was mostly square dancing. Once in a while, they'd play a slow number, but mostly fast square dancing."

Uncle Herman and Aunt Hilda were listening, too. He came to the country club dances, he said, to be seen and to make business contacts. Aunt Hilda said she was lucky if he would dance one dance with her per evening.

"What kind of people came to the honky-tonk?" Darlene asked.

"Well, about like what you'd expect. Soldiers and boys like me, who soon would be soldiers. Men running around on their wives. Some divorced women looking for a new husband, and it was a bad place to be looking. And some out-and-out whores, I guess."

"I prefer the term prostitute," Darlene said. "And did you dance with any of them?"

"Oh yes, I was a dancing fool back then. Especially when I'd had a drink or two of white likker."

"Well, we don't need any white whiskey to drink, but I'd like some punch."

"I can take a hint," I said, and promptly headed toward the end of the ballroom where they had the punch table set up. Uncle Herman went with me.

"That's a sweet little girl you've got there," he said. "But she sure is feisty."

WILLARD, UNCLE Jubal's youngest brother, had stood right in the middle of the floor that night and refused at first to let Jubal hold on to the red straw.

"It ain't right, brother," he said. "I'll do it. Gimme that straw."

"No, Willard, it's my duty," Uncle Jubal had said, staring at the straw like it had some sort of mystical powers. "It must be God's will."

None of us could argue with him on that. He had the inside track with the Good Lord and we knew it.

I said, "I'll help all I can. What do we do now?"

"I'll tell you what to do now," Jubal said. "Let's each one put twenty dollars in the pot to buy the gun with and we'll send some of the women to buy it. Get me a repeater, my eyes ain't as good as they used to be. I might miss the first shot—need something that'll shoot several times."

"My Flossie has learnt to drive, got her driver's license," Willard said. "And I bought a Chevrolet, 1939 model, couple of months back from a fellow over in town. Flossie can drive it real good."

"We'll send Alma with her and they can go to Wilmington," Jubal said. "Alma's got some kin that lives at Scotts Hill there, just out of Wilmington, give them women a good excuse to be going."

"When they need to go?"

"Next week would be good," Willard said. "Flossie's canning beans and stuff in the garden right now. Our garden was late this year, on account of the little rain we got early in the summer, but it's coming in good now and we like to have a lot of vegetables and stuff put up for the winter."

"It's good for a woman to can stuff. Willard, you got a good'un there."

"She can sew too," Willard said. "Flossie's real smart with her hands."

They nodded in group appreciation of a wife with skills.

"I feel real sorry for that June," he said, suddenly changing the conversation. "Wes, didn't you say you went to see her? Is she making it all right by herself?"

"She was cooking something for herself," I told them, "but she looked like life was pretty hard on her." I told them that we might sue Frog for the wreck, told them about the photographs, maybe told too much.

"Well, when we get done with him, he ain't gonna be around for you to sue," Jubal said. "Let's get the money together and we'll send the women next week for the gun. I don't know nothing about buying guns—where they gonna get it?"

"They got a big Montgomery Ward store in Wilmington," one of the middle brothers said. "You can get anything you want in there, I guess. Or you could go to a pawn shop."

"Hire somebody off the street to buy it for you."

"Have them women tell the clerk they're buying it for a present. To give to their man for Christmas."

"That might work. It ain't but about three months 'til Christmas."

"They need to get some shells too, some buckshot."

"Boys, we've got to remember the seriousness of this," Jubal said. "We're going to take a man's life here, for the good of the community. Think about it. Every man has got to do his part and we've got to keep quiet about it. Don't tell nobody but your wife. If anybody talks, we could all go to the pen, or the gas chamber."

We all got real quiet on that. North Carolina wasn't reluctant to execute folks—black or white—and we all knew it. And we had all seen Frog Cutshaw perform magic with that .45 automatic. He could shuck it out in the open and have it spitting lead faster than any pistol instructor at Parris Island, faster than any Marine raider I had ever seen in action.

TURKEY JACK came to the law office to get me.

"Since we be partners," he said, "I want you to see what a fine job I got us on now, look at your investment."

"Where we going?"

"I'll do the driving, take you out and bring you back," he said. "It's out in the swamp, not far from where I live, but yore little car'll never make it on the road we have to travel. Come on." We climbed in a truck I immediately recognized as one of my dad's old ones.

"Still runs good," Jack said, "and we get a lot of use out of that old tractor. Beats the hell out of horses."

He drove us toward Big Carver Swamp where we left the two-lane asphalt road and turned into a muddy track recently cut through the woods into the blackwater swamp.

"Muddy road, just like I remember in the old days."

"Yeah, Wes, things ain't changed much. Me and yore daddy, those were good days."

"Black water and black dirt, slick as owl shit. I don't see how you get vehicles in and out of here."

"We just do what we have to do. Both the trucks got good rough treads on the back, and we kin put chains on 'em if we have to."

"What do you do when you get stuck? I mean buried in the mud with a load of logs on?"

"That's when yore old tractor comes in handy. We can pull the truck out with the tractor, if the cable don't break."

"Yeah, I remember that part of logging. Even as a boy I was terrified of cables. A tight cable can break, tight as a banjo string, and snap a man in half."

"One of the most dangerous things there is, Junior, you got that right. But logging itself is always dangerous. Tree can fall the wrong way."

He got quiet then, realizing what he'd said. My thoughts went back to Dad and the way he'd died, typical logging luck. Turkey Jack had been with him that day, had walked out to the truck with my father's lifeless body in his arms they said, tears streaming down his cheeks. Nobody had ever seen Turkey Jack cry, before or since.

"I loved yore daddy, Junior. He treated me like a man, never talked bad to me. We ate together, fought the world together, cut down the biggest trees you ever saw. One time I got sick back in the woods and he put me to bed and nursed me, brought food to me, carried me to the privy when I had to go. I still miss him."

I looked over at him, staring straight ahead and fighting the steering wheel on the old truck as he kept us in the narrow, rutted road. He was a living legend among the loggers in White County, this lean muscled mix of Indian, colored and white. His old slouch hat was pulled low over his eyes, and the signature turkey feather stuck in the hatband bobbed when he moved and gave him a jaunty look.

He said, "Junior, lemme tell you about y'r daddy. I never did tell you exactly how it happened. And it's been four, five years now and I can talk about it, I think."

He recounted the incident, putting in all the details of where they were working, the timber itself. All the loggers talked like that—they were interested in the woods because that's where they lived and made their living. If they told you a story, it would be punctuated with references to the pines or gum or black oak that was vital to their story, at least in their own minds.

"We were cutting on a big old cypress," Jack said. "He was pulling his end of the saw and I was pulling mine. We had opened up a good cut, drove a pair of wedges in behind the blade and had it going our way. Almost through it when he said, 'Jack, les stop fer a minute and get a drink of water.' It was a granddaddy tree, one of the real old ones, and it was hard work putting that crosscut through it.

"So we stopped and had us a drink of good spring water we'd took in there with us, in a fruit jar, both of us drinking out of the same jar. Yore daddy never put hisself above anybody; reason we all liked him so good.

"Then we pitched back to sawing, back and forth, back and forth. Blade was getting a little dull now but it was almost done. We heard that old tree cracking and groaning way up inside it, above our heads, but we never thought nothing of it 'cause lots of them would creak and pop when they went down.

"It started leaning over to fall and that's when it happened. We never knew it, but there was a big long rotten place inside the tree, like a cave or something, but it was hidden behind the bark. That made it weak right above where we was cutting.

"When it started to fall, instead of falling away from us like we planned, the rotten place gave way and the whole butt section of that big tree splintered in two pieces. Some of it kicked back my way, just barely missed me, and the biggest part of the tree just come straight down like it was trying to re-plant itself in the ground.

"Yore daddy never had a chance. It crushed him in an instant, and then it sorta bounced off him, as the crown of the tree came over and down. If it hadn't, I couldn't have got it off him. But when it finally come to rest, there he lay in the clear. And I knowed he was dead."

He looked over at me then and smiled and shook his head. "I'm sorry, Wes, I wish it had been me."

I told him it was all right, I knew he did everything he could. We were getting into the camp now. The shacks, the machinery lying about, it brought back a lot of memories.

"Some of these boys stay out here for weeks at a time," Jack said. "And I stay out here, too, but I have to go to town to get food for 'em or parts for the trucks or the tractor. We cook and work and sleep—we like it out here."

An old black man came out to greet me, said he was too old to pull a crosscut saw. So Fred, that was his name, did most of the cooking and also sharpened the saws for the loggers.

"Fred, tell Wes how you sharpen the steel," Jack said.

"Well, sir, it 'pends on what trees they cuttin' down."

He showed me his files and tools, explaining that if the saw men were cutting mostly pine, he would set the teeth on the saw at a certain angle to take advantage of the soft pine. If they were cutting in hardwoods, it took a different angle to make the sawteeth work to best effect.

"Fred's been with me a long time," Jack said. "He's a good cook, too. But I got something out here he won't cook for us. Don't know why."

Fred rolled his eyes, shook his head and went back to his saw filing. Jack led me over to a rusty barrel. "Look in there," he said, grinning and gesturing down in the barrel.

I looked in the darkness and at first could see nothing. It was sitting in the shade and there was nothing but shadow in the bottom of the metal barrel. Then my eyes adjusted to the light and could make out something—a lump at one side of the bottom.

"Les drag it out here in the light," Jack said, grabbing the top rim of the barrel and pulling it into the full sunlight. I looked in again and could now plainly see a snake in the bottom. Jack's eyes met mine, proud of his trophy.

"Cottonmouth. Caught him out in the swamp the first day we were here."

"Jack, you ought to let that thing go. It might get out and bite somebody."

"If it gets out, it'll probably go back to the water. But it ain't getting out."

"They say a cottonmouth will come after you, the only snake that will charge you, try to bite you. Is that true?"

"Yeah, if you devil one and make it mad, they'll get after you. I caught that one asleep; had him before he knowed what was going on."

We didn't talk about it anymore after that. I could see it all. Turkey Jack would catch and keep a snake just because that's the kind of man he was. The fact that he had killed other men in hand-to-hand fights was well known. The fact that he kept a poisonous snake in a barrel tended to keep his men in awe of him, respectful. He never had to threaten to put one of his men in the barrel with the snake—it was never even mentioned. But it was always in the back of their minds.

"Wes, we got a good operation here. Look at that pile of logs we've already skidded out of the woods. Running both trucks every day to the sawmill, it's gonna take months to cut out what we've got here. And that's what I want to talk about," he said, "and I wanted you to see for your ownself. I'm working one white boy out here now, and he's sorta simple-minded but he's a good strong worker. The rest of my men is all colored, and I can get all the colored loggers I want. The Army is taking a few colored but most of 'em are looking for work and I can take my pick.

"We can do better if we get us a little sawmill. Right now, we cut down trees, drag 'em out to a log landing and load 'em on a truck. We haul the logs to a sawmill and sell'em right there. The mill pays us as little as they can for our logs, then cuts 'em up and make lumber. We do the rough work and they make lumber and get rich."

"You really want to start up a sawmill?"

"Yeah, we could buy a small one and set it up here. Cut our

own logs into lumber and sell it that way."

"Where we come up with a sawmill? Where can you buy one?"

"I hear about a mill for sale every once in a while. Probably have to go a ways to get one. Haul it in here on trucks and set it up. Have to get a sawyer, a man that knows how to cut out the most lumber from a log and keep the thing running. The Army is building barracks and stuff everywhere, training men. We can sell lumber at Fayetteville, all we can get."

We wandered back over to watch old Fred filing the saws.

"Jack, that colored boy you hired off of farm work is strong enough, but he's hard to teach anything," Fred said. "The men that work with him complain about him riding the saw. He ain't learnt to just pull it when it's his turn and let the other man pull it."

"Farm boy's good and stout. He'll make a logger, give him a little time."

"Mebbe so. Hard to teach, though, like they say, you kin lead a hoss to water, but you cain't make him drink."

"If you can lead a horse to water," Jack said, pausing to spit tobacco juice in a rain puddle. "Then I say drown the sonuvabitch."

"Jack, I heard you didn't like horses. Didn't know it was that bad," I said.

"I hate the damn things. Me and y'r dad, we used to have to skid logs out with horses. Great big dumb-ass things, they bite and kick and shit all over the place. I hate the idea of a damn horse."

"You oughta been a cowboy," Fred said, winking at me. I could sense that the old cook needled Turkey Jack from time to time. "Them cowboys love their horses."

"Screw a damn horse."

"I knowed a white boy once tried to screw a horse," Fred said, laughing openly now and warming to his subject. "Big mare hoss. He was standing on a milking stool trying to get it in her when they caught him. Over in Pender County."

"Fred, will you shut up about people that screw horses?"

Jack said.

"I never brought it up. You's the one what started talk about screwing and horses."

"Can you get us a cup of coffee? Would that be asking too much?"

"Naw, sir, coffee coming right up." Old Fred winked at me again. He obviously enjoyed verbally harassing Turkey Jack.

"Talking about horses makes me think about the old days," Jack said. "I ain't never going back to logging with horses, or steam engines neither. Me and y'r daddy, we had an old Frick steam rig once, strong enough to pull down the moon if you coulda got a cable hooked to it. But that's too old and slow now. If I can find us a little sawmill to buy, it'll have some sort of a gas engine for power."

"I WANT TO talk about us," Darlene said.

It was my favorite part of our dates, when I took her home and we sat in the car and kissed before I walked her to her door. Sometimes we kissed a lot.

"Wes, talk to me," she said, pushing me away. I loved to kiss her and most nights she was willing, but tonight was different. "Tell me what's going to happen with us."

"Come here, honey," I said, and kissed her again. Her mouth was so sweet and warm, but she pulled back in a moment.

"Wes, do you love me?"

"You know I do. You're the prettiest girl I've ever seen. C'mere now."

"I know what you want. But what I want to know is, do you really love me?"

I got another kiss then but I could tell she was serious. Marriage had never come up in our conversations and I hadn't thought about it much. I just wanted to be with her and at times like this, it was painfully apparent.

"Tell it to go down," she insisted.

"Darlene . . ."

"I'm going in before something happens."

"I'll walk you to the door."

"All right, come on, but right now."

One more long, lingering kiss under the front porch light at her parent's home and our date was over.

"See you tomorrow," she whispered, and I knew everything was all right.

The full moon was shining so bright I hardly needed headlights to drive by, but I headed the Dodge coupe toward my place at the edge of town. I had heard folks say that the moon can be so bright you can read a newspaper by its light. I didn't believe that, but it was bright, bathing the town streets in a soft glow.

She hadn't visited my house, but had made comments about it a time or two, how she could plant some flowers and do some painting and make it look better. Domestic stuff that I had ignored, at least until now.

Uncle Herman hadn't pushed me to do anything, but always in the back of the conversations with him, it had been assumed that if I wanted to follow the law profession, it would mean going back to college, and then law school.

A wife wouldn't necessarily complicate any plans like that, even plans that hadn't been formally made. And I knew people got married, men acquired wives—it was just something I had never thought about as it pertained to me individually.

I had a little money. Turkey Jack was making money for me, and Uncle Herman paid me for working at his office. I would have to give it more thought.

The situation out at Caney Fork bothered me a lot and I had deliberately kept it in the back of my mind, preferring not to think about it. My God-fearing Uncle Jubal was intent on killing Frog Cutshaw and was leading us all to it. I was tied up in that and I knew it.

It was wrong in a way, but it sure felt right the way Uncle Jubal explained it and read it out of the Bible. Frog Cutshaw was an evil man, so evil that he'd have to be executed for the good of the Caney Fork community. I knew back in the old days, the men of the town or the rural settlements had done things like that, hanged bad ones when they needed hanging.

But working with Uncle Herman, even seeing how the law works behind the scenes, I knew that killing somebody was against the law.

You might say I was caught between my two uncles.

But I had already made up my mind to help Uncle Jubal, do anything that had to be done to bring it about. He and Aunt Alma had partially raised me out on the farm, so I owed them a lot.

A little after midnight, I drove the coupe into my own yard, cut the switch off and climbed out in the moonlight. As soon as the car door shut behind me, I heard a pop from somewhere and there was a burst of energy in the dirt at my feet. Dirt and gravel stung my legs.

Then another pop and I was aware of gravel hitting the side of the car. Somebody was shooting at me!

I ran toward the house with bullets hitting all around me Aware that my hip wound was slowing me down, I ran in a funny gait that included skipping and hopping on my good leg, but I managed to cover the ground pretty fast. The shooter seemed to be standing in the shadows, underneath a big walnut tree. I was aware of the flash of his gun, like small firecrackers going off repeatedly in the shade of that tree.

Expecting to be hit any second, I reached the unlocked front door and was glad I never locked my house Nobody in Carverville did, as far as I knew. I got my hand on the doorknob and heard glass breaking as a slug took out the center pane of the nearest window. Who was after me? Were there others inside the house waiting for me?

I didn't own a gun. The only weapon in the house was that old rebel sword I had hung over the door. Would it be there? Had they already found it and now waited for me, to hack me to death with it?

I got into the house, slammed the door behind me, hearing a bullet splat against the door as it shut. I fumbled above the door, and found the sword. It felt good. I took the presence of the sword to mean that nobody was in the house. Maybe wrong, maybe right.

I backed up against the front wall right beside the door and waited, the sword held high like a baseball batter's stance. I had seen a Jap on Makin Island behead one of our men with a samurai sword—a blade at close range can be a fearsome thing.

My plan was to take the shooter if he came through the door, swinging the old saber in a good horizontal path, trying for his neck. My second lick would be to try and stab him through the body, then I'd run like hell!

It was a good plan, best I could do under the circumstances.

Nine

"SO YOU GOT shot at Saturday night?" the sheriff asked.

"Yes sir, and I'd like someone to come out and take a look."

The sheriff looked hard at me but said to go back home and a deputy would be along in a little while to investigate the incident.

I went by the law office, told Uncle Herman about it Monday morning and drove back home. Uncle Herman shook his head, as puzzled as I was.

The deputy arrived in about an hour, driving an old Ford police car that he said had been used hard by the Carverville Police before he got it.

"But it's got a bulletproof windshield," he said. "Take a look at that, about two inches thick. Po-lice department got it new in '37 and drove the wheels off it. We got it from them 'bout six months ago. Burns a lot of oil, but it gets me there and gets me back. Who shot at you?"

It was an obvious question, I knew, but it sounded funny. I told him I had no idea.

"You been screwing anybody's wife lately?"

"No, sir."

"That'll get you shot at, fer damn sure. It always does. Well, not always. But you know what I mean."

"Yes, sir."

"I'll look around and take some measurements, write up a report. You may have to help me some.

"I been up about all night," he said.

I supposed he had been working some law enforcement matter, maybe a fire or another shooting or something like that.

"No, nothing like that," he said. "I couldn't sleep a wink last night on account of that chicken liver casserole."

"What?"

"You ever eat at that diner down by the railroad?"

"Once or twice, but not regular."

"Well, I eat down there a lot. The train men all eat in there and they have good food. The cook learnt to cook, they say he did anyway, on a chain gang down in Georgia. He's not from around here."

"A chicken liver casserole?"

"Yeah, about once a week he makes a casserole with fried chicken livers in it and crumbled-up cornbread and whole grains of corn, you know, all mixed together. It's got melted cheese on top of it—it's real good."

"Never heard of anything like that."

"Well, I don't think it was the casserole, but it might have been the slaw. He puts chopped-up tomatoes in his slaw and it's good too, but I think the cabbage might have been rank. You know, starting to get too ripe fer eating."

He leaned against the side of his vehicle and I thought he was going to puke. He didn't, but he belched twice real loud, rolled his eyes and belched again.

"Where was you standing or sitting or whatever when the shooting started?"

"I was getting out of my car, about here."

I showed him where I had run, bullets hitting around me, onto the porch and into the house. He got a steel tape measure from his car and made a little drawing. We found where two bullets had made furrows in the ground and were sketching the hits when Uncle Herman and Darlene drove up.

"Oh, honey, I was so worried." She ran to me and hugged me hard, right there in front of the deputy and Uncle Herman. "When I heard about it, I had to come."

I got her quieted down and showed them all how I had run into the house, got my rebel saber and waited at the door for an entrance by the shooter that never came. The deputy got out his pocketknife and dug out two slugs, one from the door and one from the living room wall where the bullet that broke the window had finally lodged.

"It's just a .22," he said. "They don't usually kill people, but they can. Especially when it's a .22 rifle doing the shooting, and that's what this looks like."

We went out to the tree where I had seen flashes from the gun and found six shiny brass empties, all .22 caliber spent shells just like the deputy predicted.

"It was a rifle," he said. "Too far for a pistol. Some sort of repeater, and he got off half a dozen shots. Looks like he should have hit you at least once or twice."

"You sound like you're sorry he didn't hit Wes," Darlene said. Her voice was strong, she was mad and the deputy got flustered.

"I didn't mean nothing, ma'am. Just saying if the man with the rifle missed that many times, either he's a bad shot or he never meant to hit this fellow in the first place."

We went back in my house and Darlene asked for a broom, to sweep up the glass on the floor from the broken window. I had to admit that I didn't have a broom.

"Well, we're going to buy a broom and clean this mess up," she said. "And I'm going to make you some curtains—your house needs a lot of help."

I sensed the domestic tone of voice again, the home nesting instincts coming out in her. We'd be talking about the future again real soon. I could see that coming.

"I'm going to the drugstore to get something for my stomach," the deputy said. "Then I'll report to the sheriff. Y'all ever try that chicken liver casserole at the railroad diner?"

"Chicken livers?" Darlene said. "I think I'm going to gag."

"WES, WE WANT you to come out for supper," Uncle Jubal said. "Your aunt has made an apple pie. Can you come out tonight?"

I could tell by Uncle Jubal's tone of voice that he was still nervous about using a telephone and that there was probably something afoot about the planned execution of Frog Cutshaw. I said yes.

On the way out to Caney Fork, my thoughts went back over what was happening. It was puzzling—somebody had tried to kill me a few nights ago at my own house, left .22 slugs all over the place, and as far as I knew, I didn't deserve this kind of treatment.

Was it Frog Cutshaw? He'd hated me from the first, mainly because of my kinship to Uncle Jubal, I thought. But there had been some talk about his attempts to date Darlene. She had never gone out with him and now she was dating me steadily. Was that enough to get me killed?

Turkey Jack ran a rough crew of loggers and it was no secret that he and I were partners. Drinking and gambling were the main vices in a logging camp and, ironically, the main interests of a few of the men. Jack ran a tight camp and he told me he had fired two or three men over the summer. I had no personal contact with any of the men he hired or fired, didn't even know their names except for the old cook Fred.

But jobs were scarce and the loggers were a tough breed of men, given to violence. Could it be one of these, mad at Jack and me, who decided to get drunk and get even last Saturday night? And there was this matter of killing Frog Cutshaw. Uncle Jubal was certain and sure about it—he was the family leader and I respected him. I was sure he was a man of God and a deacon in the Caney Fork church. If he said Frog needed to die, then that was final and I could accept it.

But on the other hand, it was a touchy situation. I hadn't talked with Uncle Herman about it—these were two different sides of my family and I dealt with both of them, but they didn't have contact with each other. Uncle Herman routinely took on the defense of people charged with murder, and I was well aware of the law, and would someday, I hoped, be a lawyer myself and defend murderers.

And here I was, planning a killing that seemed justified, but the law would certainly see it as murder.

"Come here and let me hug you," Aunt Alma said. She always hugged me when I entered the big farmhouse. She smelled of the kitchen, and the odor of the apple pie was gentle throughout the house. She pulled my head down close and whispered. "We got the gun, honey. Jubal will tell you all about it."

The three of us sat down to a big country supper with fresh-baked biscuits. I slathered the butter and jelly on the hot biscuits and just about didn't have any room for the pie.

"Have you ever heard of a casserole made with chicken livers?" I asked.

"That's disgusting," Aunt Alma said. "Where in the world did you hear about something like that?"

"A deputy sheriff told me."

"Why are you talking to a deputy sheriff?"

"Somebody tried to kill me; shot at me last Saturday night when I came home."

"Oh, Wes, that's awful. Are you all right?"

"Yeah, I never got hit. But it sure got my attention."

"I'd say it did. Who would shoot at you?"

"Don't know, cain't figure it out. But anyway, the deputy came to investigate."

"And he told you about the chicken livers?"

"Yes ma'am, said it made him sick."

"I would think it would. Jubal likes the gizzards to eat, but nobody in this house will eat the livers so I throw 'em out to the dogs."

"Chicken livers make good bait for catfish," Uncle Jubal said.

It was about the first thing he'd said. He was a hearty eater, but not much on conversation at the table. "Hard to keep 'em on the hook, but catfish love chicken livers."

"Are you going to spend the night with us, Wes?" Aunt Alma asked.

"No, I guess not."

"Honey, it's starting to rain. That old road back to Carverville will be muddy tonight."

"I'll be all right. I won't drive fast."

I wondered if the rifleman would be waiting at home for me tonight. Did he watch my goings and comings? Was it a neighbor? I didn't have real close neighbors but there was a house less than a quarter-mile from me.

An old man lived alone in that house, and I never spoke to him, couldn't even remember his name. He and my dad had gotten into a property dispute over a boundary line, Dad had told me, years ago.

Now I owned the property, our old house that I lived in plus the land up to the disputed line. I had never even thought about it, but having bullets fired at you can get you to thinking. That old man, a veteran of World War I, might be the one.

"Looks like it's setting in to rain all night," Uncle Jubal said. "Let's go upstairs. The others'll be along in a minute or two."

Willard and the other two brothers came in, right on time, and we gathered in the same bedroom upstairs.

On the washstand table that Uncle Jubal used for a desk was his Bible and a shiny blued pump shotgun. We all stared at it.

"Boys, let's pray first," Uncle Jubal said, and began to pray, thanking God for the good rain we were getting, the crops and everything. He asked God's blessing on our effort to rid the community of an evil man, a man who had violated a woman and had killed her husband. We all said "amen" when he got through.

"Is everybody still agreed that this is the right thing to do?" he asked. "I don't have no doubts, but I don't want any of y'all to have bad feelings about this. I think we're doing our duty, got no choice."

They all nodded and I did, too. Uncle Jubal looked each one of us right in the eye and we voted with our expressions. Frog Cutshaw had been condemned.

"Right here's the gun. Pick it up and see if it suits you. Wes, you're gonna have to show me how to use it. I never owned nothing but an old single-barrel downstairs, won't shoot but one time."

I picked it up and looked it over. It was a Winchester Model 12, just like the one I had used on Makin Island, as a Marine raider, except this one didn't have a sling on it.

"The women went to Wilmington and bought it in a pawn

shop. They got a colored man on the sidewalk, paid him to go in and buy it so nobody never saw them. He got five shells for it too, buckshot.

"They sat right there in the car and waited. Nobody but that colored fellow ever saw them. I told 'em they did good."

Willard said, "Jubal you need to shoot it a time or two, see if it suits you."

"I will," Uncle Jubal said, "that won't lift no eyebrows around here. I shoot at snakes and crows and stuff every once in a while, as long as I just shoot it once or twice it won't matter if anybody hears it."

"I can show you how to shuck it fast," I said. "We'll grease it up real good so it'll spit buckshot so fast you won't believe it. Any pump gun would do, but this is a Winchester just like the ones we used against the Japs. It'll do the job."

"When we gonna do it, Jubal?"

"I figure Monday morning. I'm not going to do it on the Lord's day and there'll be too many people stirring around on Saturday morning."

"How about the foot log?" Willard asked. "I want to get my part done in plenty of time."

"We don't want a log, we want a foot plank. A log would be too heavy to move," Uncle Jubal said. "Y'all get a long plank and nail a two-by-four vertical underneath it for support. I don't want to fall in the creek, so make it stout."

They grinned, but that was about the only humor I saw that night. This was deadly serious business.

"Willard, you get the foot plank ready and you can put it in place Sunday evening. I don't want it to be there long in case somebody might see it. After I do the shooting, I'll come back across the creek to my own farm and pull the plank into the bushes so y'all can take it away Monday morning, right quick."

"How about the gun?"

"This repeater shotgun is going right back to Wilmington as soon as we can get the women ready to drive again; probably a day or two after it's done. It'll be hid in an attic in somebody's house where they'll never think to look."

"Sometimes comes down from his side of the creek to feed them hogs hisself, don't he?" Willard asked.

"Yep, that's right," one of the other brothers said. "He thinks the world of that big boar hog he calls Big Boy. He'll open up that store about daylight, leave that colored boy Reuben in charge of the store and drive down into that creek bottom to check over his hogs."

"I thought about having one o' y'all kill one of them little pigs and cut its head off, nail it to the front porch of the store," Uncle Jubal said. "That would really get him. He'd come down boiling mad for sure."

"What if the colored boy comes with him? What if there are two men in that truck when it drives down in there?" one of the others asked.

"I'm not going to kill an innocent man," Uncle Jubal said. "If that happens, like Willard said, we'll just wait until a better day. But for now, I think Monday morning is it.

"And if I don't see any of you before then, I'm counting on the foot-plank being in place Sunday night."

We all shook hands and they faded away into the rainy night.

I told Uncle Jubal I would return on Saturday morning to show him how to use the gun and oil it for him. Despite Aunt Alma's pleading to stay the night, I drove back to Carverville in a hard storm, mud splattering against the running boards of the coupe.

It had almost quit by the time I drove into my yard, just a slow steady drizzle. I turned off the headlights and sat in the car for a few moments, wondering if the shooter was waiting for me.

Turned out he was, but I had no idea at the time. He was waiting locked up inside a crude cage in the Big Carver Swamp, but I wouldn't know the details until the next day.

I tiptoed through the dark wet yard and slept like a log, with the steady raindrops pattering on the tin roof.

"IT'S FRIDAY THE thirteenth," Uncle Herman's receptionist

said. "Better watch out today, might be unlucky."

She was young and pretty, too. If it weren't for Darlene, I might be looking at her.

"You and Darlene going out tomorrow night? I bet you are, Wes. I already know the answer to that."

The secretary's underground network in Carverville knows all, I thought, *tells all and doesn't miss a trick. Now she'll start the questioning, trying for a tidbit she can pass along.*

"You gonna give her a ring, Wes? Huh, a big diamond engagement ring sometime?"

"Yeah, I'll give her a ring."

"Really? When?"

"I'll call her on the phone this morning."

"I don't mean that kind of a ring, Mr. smarty-pants."

She handed me a sheaf of papers and I went in my little office to look them over. Deeds, timber rights, easements, all legal entanglements on a thousand-acre tract over on Cape Fear. The heirs were now in a bitter fight over the property and Uncle Herman represented one side of the row.

"It's a mess," he said. "Brothers and sisters fighting each other over family land. One old sister lived in the main home place. She is still alive, but just barely. She was supposed to get the house and the biggest, best part of the land."

"She got a husband, any children?"

"No, the old country way of doing it was that the youngest child, boy or girl, wouldn't marry, even if they wanted to. They would stay with the old folks, their parents, 'til they both passed. Then that youngest child would get the home place for doing their duty."

"Never heard of that."

"Well, you were raised in town and in logging camps. You never were immersed in the country culture, even though you spent time out at Caney Fork with your dad's sister. You know, Jubal's people."

"Go on, I'm learning. You might say this is part of my legal school."

"You got a good attitude, Wes. Lots of young people won't

even listen to an older person talk. As I said, the youngest child had to stay with the parents and, in turn, would get the biggest part of the inheritance when they were dead and gone. This old sister was set to do that and the family had agreed . . . depends on your source as to how much they agreed. What tore up the pea patch, as they say, was that the oldest brother wanted part of the best land, which was located right on the home place tract."

"And she wouldn't give it up, right?"

"Not only that, but she produced a handwritten will from her mama which gave the whole damn farm to her and her alone, leaving out the other three children entirely. And if that wasn't bad enough, the reason she produced that highly questionable will was to support her action. She sold off a portion of the land that was supposed to be going to the oldest brother, just to spite him."

"Whose side are we on in this fight?"

"The oldest brother, who has been cheated in my opinion. A lawyer over in Pender County took the old sister's case and is defending her so-called will and the sale of the land. My client and his sister are on the opposite side. We contend that both the will and the deed she gave for the land she sold are fraudulent."

"What do you want me to do?"

"The old sister's mind is sharp, but her body is fading. She's being kept right here in Carverville in a house where there are nurses to help her. The farm, of course, is way down in the southeast corner of our county."

"I know where the Cape Fear River is."

"Of course you do. I know I get wordy at times. It's the way of a lawyer. What I need you to do is go down there and go in that old house."

"Anybody live there now?"

"No, they boarded it up when the old sister left, on her orders. It's got POSTED signs and NO TRESPASSING notices nailed up on all the trees in the yard. She doesn't want her family or anybody else going in the house."

"You want me to break into the house, then . . . ?"

"That's such a crude way to put it. We must learn to be

more discreet, both in our words and our actions. I would hope a violent entry wouldn't be necessary, but do what you must to get inside the old home place.

"I want you to go in and search it thoroughly, from top to bottom. Do it carefully, so it looks as if nothing has been disturbed. I don't know what you'll find, if anything. But if there was a good will, you might find it. At the very least, you should come away from there with samples of the old sister's handwriting, which we can compare to this fake will her attorney has.

"Today is Friday, so I don't expect you to do it today. And you shouldn't plan to do it on Saturday or Sunday. Country people work like the devil five days a week, but they'll come to town on Saturday or in other ways take a break from their labors. They loaf on Sunday too, even if they don't go to church. Your best bet to sneak in that old house will be Monday, when everybody goes back to regular work routines."

So there I was, a fledgling legal assistant making plans to burglarize an old country house on Monday morning. The same morning my beloved uncle would be killing a man at Caney Fork for the good of the community.

Deep in thought over this rather bizarre calendar of events, I heard a soft knock on the door and saw Turkey Jack Lowery slip into my office.

"Come on with me, Junior," he said. "I want to take you out to the camp in the swamp. I've got the man that shot at you."

Ten

"I CAUGHT HIM yesterday,." Turkey Jack said. "That little yellow bastard, started to kill him right then."

"Slow down, Jack," I said. "You're talking too fast."

"He talked too much his own self. Told some people he really made a white boy jump last Saturday night. Told it to the wrong man and it come right to me."

"Who'd you say it is? I didn't catch it the first time."

"It's Reuben, that boy helps Frog Cutshaw in the store out at Caney Fork."

"Why would he shoot at me?"

"Ask me, ol' Frog sent him to do it. Only answer I kin think of. I'm gonna let you talk to him, then I'm gonna kill him."

"No, Jack, I appreciate it, but I can't let you do that. You'll get in trouble."

"Wes, he's a dead colored. Count on that."

We stopped talking then and he drove the old truck over the muddy road into the camp. All the loggers were working; only the cook Fred was there.

"I'll take you to him," Fred said, looking sternly at Jack and me. There was no banter, no joshing with Turkey Jack today. "Jack's got 'im in a pen down here where we used to keep a mean dog."

He led me behind the loggers' shanties to a crude wooden cage, hammered together from mismatched weathered boards. It was about four feet square and maybe three feet tall. A man would have had to enter crawling on hands and knees and could only sit up in a cramped position; standing was out of the question.

"Look in there," Fred whispered. "Jack's a hard man and he thinks the world of you. This boy's gonna die and he knows it. It tears me up to think about it."

The boards which made the walls had spaces between them and I could see movement inside the cage, but I wanted to confront the shooter. Jack wasn't with us at the moment, having apparently gone to the cook shack for his ever-present cup of coffee, which was a part of him morning, noon or night.

"Open the door, I want to see him and talk to him," I said

"Jack might get me for opening the door."

"Well, get out of the way and I'll do it."

"He's tied up like a hog. He cain't run."

I opened the door and looked into the face of a light-colored man I had forgotten. Sure enough, I remembered seeing him at the store. Younger than me, maybe eighteen at the most. Tears had stained the dirt on his cheeks, and he apparently thought I was going to kill him now.

"Please, mister, don't hurt me."

Touched by his pleading eyes, I reached into the dog coop and grasped the front of his denim work shirt and pulled him out to me. He was trembling and shaking visibly, his mouth moving but not making a sound.

"Calm down, I just want to talk to you. Why in the world did you shoot at me?"

"'Cause he's a sorry bastard that works for Frog Cutshaw," Turkey Jack said, walking up with a cup of steaming coffee in his hand. "That's why he done it and that's why he's gonna die."

The youth rolled his eyes from Jack to me and back again and I could see questioning him would be impossible if Jack stayed. His wrists were bound together with leather straps and also his ankles. He stood shaking before me and I wanted answers.

"Jack, I thank you for everything you've done for me, but I want to talk to this boy alone. You understand? He's scared to death of you and I can't get anything done as long as you're standing there. You and Fred go somewhere else, leave me here with him for a few minutes. Okay?"

Jack took a long drink of his coffee, and considered my request without speaking for it seemed like a full minute before he spoke. "Wes, you be careful with him. If he tries anything, just holler and we'll come running. Nigger, I'll tell you how you gonna die. Just so you'll know. You seen that cottonmouth I keep in the barrel when I brought you in here yesterday? I'm gonna stick you headfirst down in that barrel on top of the snake and it's gonna strike you in the face, maybe two, three times. Then I'm gonna let the poison work on you. When you swell up and the skin starts splitting open on your head, I'm gonna cut yore throat and leave you out in the swamp somewhere. When the coons and the minks and the gators get through eating on you, there won't be nothing left but some scattered bones for the buzzards to peck on.

"And you won't be the first I've done like that," Jack said, turned on his heel and walked away. Fred helped me hoist Reuben onto the roof of the coop and he sat there, looking downward. Fred patted me on the shoulder and followed Jack back toward the cook shack.

"I never been in a swamp in my whole life," Reuben said as I strained to hear him. His voice was low and sad, but he spoke freely, relieved that Jack was no longer threatening him. "And now it looks like I'll die here. Always been afeared o' the swamp. They say there's Indian haints out here and gators as big as a horse and snakes and stuff. Lord help me now."

I let him talk and I listened. The question I had would be answered soon enough.

"My mama always said she was afraid I would die early. Looks like she was right. I'm caught between the two meanest men in this whole country, Mr. Frog Cutshaw and Mr. Turkey Jack Lowery. It don't matter which way I go, one of 'em's gonna kill me.

"Mr. Jack's gon' kill me for shooting at you. And I never meant to hit you, God's truth, I swear. I just wanted to do it so word would get back to Mr. Frog and he'd know I done it. I onliest done it to satisfy him. I knowed he'd cuss at me fer missing you, but he'd be satisfied for the time being and maybe I'd be off the hook. But he might kill me yet. I ain't sleeping very well these days, I know too much."

"What do you know too much about?"

"Them black-market t'ars he sells out there. I'm the one that puts 'em on folks' cars and trucks. They come in there at night from all over, 'specially when he gets in a truckload o' fresh ones. Pay big money to get new t'ars."

"Frog wouldn't kill you over tires, would he?"

"How about that pore Army man he run over? I was with him in the truck that day—it never had no brake troubles. We seen that man driving toward us and Mr. Frog sez 'Hold on, bo,' and we slam right into him.

"Went back to the sto', and he made me climb under the front and loosed the brake line with a monkey wrench, made some fluid run out on the ground. When the law come, he seen the fluid on the dirt, Mr. Frog told 'im 'See there, tole you the brakes was bad.'"

"How about the woman in the store?" I asked and he dropped his gaze and shook his head.

"I don't want to talk about it," he said, and he was whispering so low I could barely hear him. Talking about sex and white women was a taboo subject that could get him killed by a white man, even by me if I was inclined. He started shuddering again and rolled his eyes. But I pressed on.

"Tell me the truth, I won't hurt you," I told him. "I already know. I just want to hear how you tell it." His eyes teared up and he whispered the story.

"The lady come in by herself," he said, "just Mr. Frog and me in the place. He grabbed her, tore off her clothes and got on her like a hog from behind. She never had a chance.

"Mr. Frog, he was laughing when it was over, but she was crying and trying to hide herself with her hands. I run outside and Mr. Frog was still laughing. Next time I seen her, she had got her clothes back on best she could and was running away from the store. It was awful but I couldn't do nothing for her."

They put him back in his rough cell and Turkey Jack drove me back to town. I made him promise me he wouldn't kill Reuben for a day or so.

SATURDAY MORNING I drove to Caney Fork bright and early, to eat a big country breakfast at Aunt Alma's table and teach Uncle Jubal the finer points of handling and shooting his new weapon.

We walked down behind the barn, in case anyone drove up while we had the new gun out. I found an old piece of plank about a foot wide and two feet long, propped it against the bottom wire of the fence.

"The ladies bought five buckshot shells," I said. "I want you to shoot one of them at that board—show me what you've got. The other four will go into the gun for the work Monday morning. Each one of these shells has got about a dozen big lead balls in it and they should fly in a good tight pattern. You'll be close to him when you let it go, so one good hit will do the job."

"Sounds good to me," Uncle Jubal said. "Only thing I don't want to do is to shoot it real fast. I shoot my old single-shot gun around here at crows and snakes and stuff, so somebody in the neighborhood that hears a shot or two from here isn't going to be suspicious."

I showed him the safety and the slide release on the Winchester and brought it to my own shoulder a time or two. It brought back all the memories from the Makin raid, the heft of the gun in my hands and the feel of putting my face to the buttstock and looking down the barrel.

"Try it yourself," I told him, "you're going to like it better than that old single-barrel."

Uncle Jubal shouldered the pump gun several times, swinging it on a passing sparrow, pointing it at the barn door, smiling and snapping it at the fence post.

"Gonna be all right," he said. "Let me try one of those buckshot loads."

I showed him how the shells would go in the tube magazine and with each pump of the gun, be fed into the chamber for firing.

"You can shoot it as fast as you can work that pump."

"I believe you," he said.

He backed off no more than twenty feet from the board,

and pulled the trigger. The buckshot pellets shredded the center of the board and plowed up the damp ground behind it, sending the target flying off into the weeds.

"Recoil's stronger than birdshot."

"That's right," I said. "But in the heat of battle, you'll never feel the recoil or even hear the gun go off."

"I'll take your word for it. Load it up for me and let me try the pumping part."

I loaded the four live rounds into the gun and warned him to hold the release and not touch the trigger. He slam-pumped the four rounds through the gun. I caught them before they could fall to the ground and get gritty.

He worked the safety again and again with the gun unloaded, until he was confident with it. Then he limped over to the wire and looked off into the weeds at the busted board. Nodding his head, he said he was ready.

"I almost forgot, Turkey Jack's got the man that shot at me."

"Tell me about it. Who was it?"

"Reuben."

"Oh, I know him. His sister and her kids work here on my place. They're the only tenants I've got right now. Why did he shoot at you?"

I told him about what Reuben said, about the wreck and about the rape scene in the store.

"Well, I was convinced that what we're doing is right," he said, "but that puts a lid on it, don't it?"

"Jack and my dad were real close—he feels like he's protecting me and I appreciate it. But I think he's planning on killing Reuben for shooting at me."

"Hold on, wait a minute and let me talk. This might work out better for us."

Ruby had had a man, not married but a steady man who lived with her and supposedly had fathered at least one of her children. The man's ability to work had been the bedrock of the tenant arrangement with Uncle Jubal, which allowed the colored family to live and work on the farm.

"But the man run off," Uncle Jubal said, "and he let Ruby and her children stay, but this arrangement isn't satisfactory because Ruby's ability to work is limited. Reuben comes to see her sometimes, mostly I guess to get some better grub than he gets living in a shack behind the store. But I can't get him to come and work on the farm for me. They've got a brother that lives up in Baltimore they talk about sometimes. I've got an idea and we'll have to move fast."

We walked back to the house and I loaded the pump gun fully for him, with one in the chamber and three rounds up the spout.

"It's on safety," I told him, "be real careful with it. All you gotta do is punch the safety off and start shucking and shooting."

He hid it in the house and came back on the back porch to send me away. "Here's a five-dollar bill, Wes. I think Reuben'll be more use to us alive than dead. He needs to get out of here and if he's gone, two good things will happen. He won't be shooting at you anymore and he won't be with Cutshaw on Monday morning, which will simplify things a lot. I want you to go get him and put him on a bus today, send him to his brother at Baltimore. This will be enough money for a one-way ticket."

I drove back to Carverville as fast as I could and went to the bus station. Sure enough, a bus from the east would wind its way through Carverville late Saturday afternoon, eventually making it to Fayetteville to the west.

"Yes," the agent said, "at Fayetteville you can get a connection to DC and on up to Baltimore."

With the bus ticket in my shirt pocket, I headed out to the swamp. The road into the camp was drivable by car for a short ways, after which I had to get out and walk on in.

Jack was nowhere in sight, the old cook Fred said, preferring to spend Saturday night with the Geechee woman at his own house. Some of the loggers had also gone home, but two of them were pitching a leisurely game of horseshoes, the steel shoes ringing loudly when they connected with the iron stobs.

"Let the boy out of the dog pen, I'm taking him with me," I said.

"Can't do that, boss. Jack'll get me for sure."

"I'm a half-owner of this outfit. Jack and me are partners. You know that?"

"Yes sir, we know."

"Get him out right now, I gotta go."

He reluctantly did as I ordered and Reuben walked out slowly to the cook shack, rubbing his hands and wrists where the leather thongs had held him.

He was nervous, but we walked out of that camp together, under the watchful stares of Fred and the horseshoe pitchers. I put him in the car, bought him a hamburger in Carverville and at 4:30 that Saturday afternoon, put him on a bus bound for Baltimore.

MONDAY MORNING came cool and clear, second week of September, 1943. I had an idea of my own and drove out toward Caney Fork real early, before daylight. Something told me that I needed to be there, hidden, in case Uncle Jubal needed me.

I didn't have a gun, didn't take the old Rebel sword or any weapon at all. But in case my crippled uncle needed help, whether he wanted it or not, I would be there. If everything went as planned, I would simply fade away into the woods and nobody would know.

Uncle Jubal was a proud man. He had drawn the red straw fair and square and was ready to do his duty alone. He wouldn't have permitted it, but I was going to be on Frog's side of the creek for the party, just to be sure.

My wounded leg was getting stronger all the time. I limped a little but certainly not as bad as Uncle Jubal with that short leg of his. And for this mission, I didn't mind getting my feet wet. I parked the coupe in a bushy woods away from the main road and headed out.

The gnats were already stirring as well as the mosquitoes. I had forgotten how miserable it could be to be work in the woods like the loggers do. Daylight was coming—I'd have to hurry to be in place.

I was on Uncle Jubal's property, paralleling the main creek and crossing the bottom edge of a big cornfield, clothes soaked with dew. I waded the creek at a place where it ran over a rock bar, the riffles covering the sound of my splashing and the little rapids making it a shallow place to cross. Then I was on Frog's land, between the creek and the road he would be coming down in a few minutes.

I hunkered down behind a big yellow pine to catch my breath, realizing I had come up on Frog's hog lot road too high and would have to walk downhill to find the place where he parked his truck when he was tending his hogs.

Then I heard the truck coming and very, very slowly peeped around the base of the pine. I was looking right into the muzzle of a rifle barrel not twenty feet away, and aiming right at me.

"No, no," I hollered but it was too late.

June stood in some thick honeysuckles right across the narrow little road from me, pointing her husband's Army carbine right in my direction.

At that moment in my left side vision I saw Frog's big truck plunging from left to right down the road and she turned that semi-automatic military carbine loose. The roaring of the truck and the rattle of rifle fire in my face made me instinctively dive for the ground.

Frog's windshield exploded in a shower of shiny glass splinters and some of her bullets thudded against the big pine over my head, raining bark chunks down on me.

The truck sped out of sight and I got to my feet, looking across the road at June. She looked amazed, our eyes locked for a moment and then she turned and walked deliberately away into the woods. I ran down the road toward the hog lot, realizing Frog would now be on full alert and mad as hell.

My running wasn't what it used to be, more like a skip, but it got me there quickly. When I got a glimpse of Frog's truck through the trees, I hit the woods and eased up on the scene.

"You sons-a-bitches," Frog screamed. He was furious, so

mad he was jumping up and down, almost foaming at the mouth. "Come on out and fight, goddamn you, I'll kill ever' goddamn one of you."

He ran around his truck, pounding his fist on the hood and making the glass remains of his windshield dance on the metal with his fury. Horrified, I saw Uncle Jubal step out of some sweet gum bushes and level the shotgun at him.

"You old bastard," Frog yelled at him, reaching with his right hand for the deadly .45. Uncle Jubal's mouth fell open and he fainted dead away, crumpling to the ground thirty feet from the rear of the truck.

"Well, ain't got the nerve, have you?" Frog said.

Frog walked over to Uncle Jubal, bent over and looked at him and put his pistol back in his rear pocket. He took the pump gun from Uncle Jubal and leaned it against the rear of his truck, looked back and started walking around the truck again.

I measured the distance in my mind and figured it to be about thirty-five feet from the tree that hid me to the shotgun propped at the truck, less than horseshoe pitching range. I couldn't run as good as I could before the Jap bullet got me, but I could run-skip the distance in a few seconds if I timed it right.

"Old man, somebody's gonna die fer this," Frog roared from the front of the truck.

I took a deep breath and started hard for the gun. I was halfway to it when Frog must have heard me. I was bending over as I ran so there was no way he could have seen me.

I got my hands on the Winchester, pushed the safety off and had it level when he came around the front left-hand corner of the big truck. His nickel-plated pistol was in his hand and it was coming up fast.

I got the first shot off, about waist-high and level. The pump jumped in my hands and the load of buckshot caught Frog in the chest. He staggered, but didn't go down and his pistol fired almost straight up as he made an effort to keep standing. I shucked the pump and shot it empty, pulling the trigger as fast as the mechanism would work. He fell backward, but the buckshot found his upper body and face until it was over.

Trembling with the adrenaline now rushing through my body, I propped the gun back against the truck and walked toward my silent Uncle Jubal. Had he died of a heart attack? Was it just too much for him? I felt for a pulse and it was there, strong and steady. I patted his cheeks firmly and squeezed his hands and he groaned. Then he opened his eyes, looked around and felt the hard ground he was lying on.

"What's happening?" he said. "What are you doing here?"

I helped him to his feet and he looked over at Frog Cutshaw, lying dead beside his truck, the deadly .45 gripped tightly in his hand.

"Let's get out of here, Uncle Jubal. We did a lot of shooting this morning. Somebody will be coming down here. We gotta go."

Eleven

"YOU CARRY THE gun and I'll get the foot plank," I said.

Uncle Jubal and I crossed the creek. I grabbed one end of the foot plank and wrestled it over on our side of the stream. Careful not to leave any marks, I picked it up and got it on my shoulder and we hurried into the cornfield. I could hear voices in the corn and my surprise must have showed on my face.

"It's all right," Uncle Jubal said. "That's Ruby and her kids pulling corn. I parked a wagon down here last week and they're gathering the corn. She's gonna be my alibi."

I hoped nobody would need an alibi, but Uncle Jubal was doing a lot of thinking about it and that was good. I didn't have an alibi, since I was being sent today to do a burglary in the lower end of the county. Legal work was so interesting.

"Hide that plank up in the woods at the upper end of the field. Willard will come and get it later this morning."

I did as he asked and also took the gun from him, stashing it temporarily beside a rotting log at the edge of the field.

"I'm gonna go talk to Ruby a minute. Wait for me here and you can ride back to the house with me. My truck's parked a little ways up that road."

He disappeared into the cornfield, and I soon heard him talking to the tenant family, but they were too far. I couldn't make out the words.

"I got Ruby off to the side and talked to her alone," he said as we reached the truck. "I told her I would be back in about thirty minutes to help her and her kids finish this field. But I wanted her to tell the sheriff, if he asks her, that I was here with them working since daylight.

"She knows something is going on. They heard the shots 'cause it's just a little ways across the creek bottom. But she seemed to be relieved to hear that Frog Cutshaw is dead. Most of the colored folks despise him because of the way he treats them. Talks bad to them all the time."

"She say anything about Reuben?"

"No, I didn't mention it and neither did she. Her oldest boy, though, he give me the bad eye. He's about thirteen and goes to school some at Carverville, you know, at the school they have for the colored over there. Smart boy, she says, gets good grades."

"You think the sheriff'll be out here today?"

"Don't know, it'll take 'em a while to sort things out."

He hid the gun in the corn crib, wrapped it up in the brown paper it had come in and covered it with loose corn. Aunt Alma hugged both of us, her eyes moist but saying nothing. I told them to be brave, that I had to go, and lit out for my hidden car.

Staying on the back roads, I was down in the end of the county near the big Cape Fear shortly before noon, sitting in the coupe and eating cheese and crackers I got at a country store. I washed it down with a Coke, which the country people still called a "dope." Aunt Hilda told me that was because the drink had contained a drug, but that it had been removed years ago. "Gimme a dope and some nabs," a rural customer would say, and the store-man would fill the order with a soft drink and snack crackers. Language intrigued me.

I found the big country house Uncle Herman wanted examined, hid the car for the second time that day and hiked in. September was still warm and this close to the river, a man could see snakes, even alligators along the canals and creeks. It was strange country to me, and I took my time working my way in.

Sure enough, the big house was boarded up and looked abandoned—weeds waist-high in the yard, paint peeling. A crow sitting in a crepe myrtle bush saw me, cawed real loud and flapped away. No other signs of life.

All the windows had been neatly covered with boards on the ground floor, but I easily went in the back door because it had been removed from its hinges. The floor creaked as I entered a back hallway and looked around. The place was a mess.

Whoever had taken down the door had been looking for the same evidence I was seeking. The house had been ransacked—drawers emptied in the floor, clothing scattered, furniture overturned. The only papers I found were on the floor near a desk on the second floor. No boards on the windows up here, noonday sun streaming in. The papers were some old photographs, a letter or two, an old calendar and some valentines and school report cards. Nothing of any use.

So I took the letters anyway, to prove I'd done as asked. The old house smelled musty, so I was glad to get out of there. I went home, took a bath and changed clothes before going to the law office.

"NOT MUCH HERE," Uncle Herman said, looking intently at the letters. "But they may be helpful. These are from the old sister to somebody—they could be used to show as samples of her handwriting. Only problem will be to show legally how we got them."

Then his mind changed gears—I could see it in his eyes as he looked right at me.

"Somebody killed Frog Cutshaw out at Caney Fork this morning. You hear about that? Know anything about it?"

"No, sir. Been down in the Cape Fear country all day, didn't talk to anybody."

"You sure?"

"Yes, sir."

Uncle Herman was a quick judge of character and he had judged some real characters in his career. But I had decided not to mix family matters.

Uncle Herman would know immediately that either I was lying to him and probably would never tell him the truth, or that I was telling the truth. Either way, the questioning would do no good. Or maybe he didn't want to know my involvement.

"Sheriff's deputies have been out there all day, haven't come back to town yet. Big crowd of people they say gathered around to see him lying there. Happened close to his store, at a hog lot."

I nodded. I could imagine the stir it made in Caney Fork. He said the rumors were flying about who did it. A colored boy that worked at the store was missing, he said, had been missing for a day or so before the shooting. And there were the black-market tires that were sold at the store, obtained from mysterious sources. Maybe they shot Cutshaw.

WE DIDN'T USUALLY go out on weeknights, but Darlene called the office right before closing time Monday afternoon. "I want to talk to you, Wes. Let's go somewhere tonight and eat and talk."

"Do you like chicken liver casserole?"

"Stop joking around. I'm not eating anything like that."

"No kidding, on a Monday night in Carverville the only place we can get supper will be down at the railroad café or over at the country club. Nobody else will be open."

"I'll take the country club."

"Don't get used to it."

"Well, I don't want to be so hard on your pocketbook, but this time I want privacy and I don't want everybody in town staring at us."

"Okay, pick you up at six. It won't take long to drive out there."

Carverville was just barely big enough to have a country club, everybody knew that. Uncle Herman was a charter member, so I came and went as I pleased, but mostly as an outsider who never felt at ease here. To the old money, I was a logger's kid who would never play golf.

"It's so pretty out here," Darlene said, snuggling over against me as we drove the entrance road to the club. "I came out here with one of my girlfriends back in the spring, when the azaleas were blooming. It looked like a picture in a magazine."

"The groundskeepers do a good job. The irrigation from these ponds they have around the course is what keeps everything so green."

"Do you eat out here much?"

"Sometimes. Herman brings me out here for lunch sometimes. They have some booths in the restaurant part, a little more private for conversation."

The restaurant was small, adjoining the bar. Technically, of course, White County was dry. Meaning that liquor or beer or wine couldn't be sold legally anywhere in the town or county. And, of course, it couldn't be legally consumed anywhere either.

But the people who owned and ran Carverville would help the preachers vote against alcohol, and then run a wide-open bar at their country club. For members only, which kept out the riffraff.

"Do you drink much, Wes? I never asked you."

"Naw, I tried it once or twice, saw a lot of drunkenness in the Marines. But it's not for me."

"Why, I bet you were funny when you were drunk."

"I might have been, but I don't like being funny. I puked in the bed one night, so drunk I couldn't stand up, and when I lay down, it seemed the bed got up with me and spun round and round. I realized that the man who told me this was fun had told me a damn lie."

"It's all right, honey, I was just saying that to be cute. I couldn't marry a drunk."

Neither of us spoke for a while after that. Marriage was a scary subject but she had said what was important to her, and it was a sobering thought.

The barman seated us in a dark-paneled booth at a corner window, overlooking the golf course. It was almost dark, the shadows from the long-leaf pines overtaking the fairways. There were only two old men drinking in the bar, no other restaurant patrons yet.

"Drinks, folks?" the waiter asked.

"Bring us two ice teas, please, and a menu."

"Coming up."

"The food is good here," I told her. "Only the best, and they don't pay any attention to the war going on. They get around the rationing just like they get around the water and electricity. Uncle Herman told me that the mayor and the town council members were all in the country club and the town's electric department had run a power line to the club house years ago that wasn't metered at all."

"In other words, they use all the electricity they want and don't pay a bill?"

"That's right, and the city water is the same way. They ran a big water line out from town, supposedly to take in some houses on the edge of town, then ran it all the way to the clubhouse. No meter, no bill."

"Well, it's not right. But we might as well enjoy it while we're here."

They brought us seafood, fresh flounder trucked in from Wilmington earlier that day. It was delicious.

"Wes, I want to talk about us," she said, when we had finished the pecan pie. She didn't drink coffee after a meal but I did, a souvenir habit from the Marines.

"Well, talk then. I'm a good listener."

She talked and talked and I let her. It was all about us, although she never did actually say the marriage word. But she told me that she wanted to go to college and be a schoolteacher, and she wanted to be a mother, too, and have children, in a little town like ours.

She prodded me about my plans, what I wanted and I babbled about someday going to law school. The war was pressing on us and we couldn't plan much until it was over, seemed to me.

"I got a letter from my old Marine buddy from North Carolina," I said. "You remember the one I told you about, we called him Hillbilly?"

"From the mountains?"

"Yeah . . . the other end of the state. He said the boy from Maine got killed. They all got shot up bad on one of those island fights. Hillbilly was wounded, like me, out of the fighting now and in a hospital in California."

"You're lucky to be alive."

"I know. But I feel guilty sometimes with them still out

there in the Pacific and me safe at home."

"It's not your fault," she said, and reached across the table to grab my hand. I looked into her face and saw some of that small-town dream she'd been talking about.

Under the front porch light at her parent's house, we kissed goodnight, a long slow kiss that promised more in the future. I was keenly aware of the pressure of her body against mine, her hair, the smell and touch of her.

"Night," she whispered. "Be careful."

I was puzzled by that, thinking about it as I drove home. She hadn't mentioned the Cutshaw matter and I had expected to be questioned about it. Now she told me to be careful.

TUESDAY MORNING, I went back to Caney Fork, to Uncle Jubal's house. I saw a strange car in the yard, but it was soon explained.

"Alma and Willard's wife going back to Wilmington," Uncle Jubal said in the kitchen. "They're getting their stuff together to go and spend the night, then come back tomorrow."

"I already put the gun under the back seat, still wrapped in the brown paper it come in. Willard come last night and took the foot plank away and burned it up on a brush pile where he's been clearing some land.

"If we can get these women on the road and away from here, I can rest easy."

Aunt Alma swept into the room, dressed in her Sunday best for the trip, and introduced me again to her sister-in-law, who smiled and said she remembered me from the last time. There was a forced air about the women. They were smiling, but it was deadly serious business and we all knew it.

The sound of motors approaching drew our eyes to the yard and Willard's wife sighed aloud as two sheriff's cars drove into view. "Dear Lord," she said, "look at that."

The sheriff and three deputies got out of the two vehicles, peered into my coupe and Willard's car.

"Good morning," Uncle Jubal said, greeting them from the

back porch steps. "What are y'all looking for?"

"Jubal, we're looking for anything to tell us what happened to Frog Cutshaw," the sheriff said, grim-faced and uncomfortable in this setting. Uncle Jubal was a respected man in the community. The sheriff ordinarily dealt more with lower folk.

"We heard about it," Uncle Jubal said. "I don't know how we could be of any help to you, but we'll be glad to answer your questions, show you anything you want to see."

"We got a search warrant. Gonna have to look in the house, the barn, anywhere we need to look. Whose cars are these?"

"One is mine."

"Yeah, I know who you are. That's your lawyer uncle's coupe ain't it?"

"Yes."

"Who's the other?" he asked.

Uncle Jubal said, "It's my brother Willard's. His wife and mine are going to Wilmington today to see some relatives."

Aunt Alma motioned to me then and I took their two suitcases out to Willard's car.

"Wait a minute," Willard's wife yelled and came out with a big armload of clean sheets and blankets. One of the deputies opened the door of the car and she piled the bedding onto the empty back seat. Then the deputy turned and let her place the two suitcases on top of the bedding.

"Don't pile it up too high," he said. "You won't be able to see out the back glass."

"Alma, we're gonna have to search your house," the sheriff said glumly. "We won't tear nothing up but we gotta look."

"Reckon we ought to look in them suitcases they're taking?" one of the deputies said.

The sheriff gave him a bad look and said, "No, we'll just look in the house."

"You help yourself, Sheriff," Aunt Alma said. "Wes and Jubal will be here if you need anything. We're going now, if that's all right."

"Sure," the sheriff said, and they drove away right under the noses of the law, with that Model 12 Winchester hidden under a car seat and a pile of bedding and two ladies' suitcases.

Of course, it had helped when Willard's wife told the deputy that she thought the relative in Wilmington was coming down with TB. I saw him flinch—even the thought of that contagious disease was scary. I could tell that the deputy standing closest to their car didn't want to search it. Don't think the sheriff heard the TB remark, but it didn't hurt any.

"Let's go look in the house," the sheriff said, and we took them in. They looked in drawers and under beds and in Aunt Alma's big wardrobe, where her dresses hung neatly. Country houses didn't have any closets.

"Where's your gun, Jubal?" the sheriff asked.

Uncle Jubal produced a single-shot, break-open 12 gauge from behind the big wood-burning kitchen stove. Aunt Alma had a new electric stove in her kitchen, but they hadn't discarded the old wood-burner either. Uncle Jubal said biscuits tasted better baked on the woodstove and he had to have his biscuits hot and fresh every morning.

The sheriff pressed the lever to open the gun and looked out through the barrel, holding it up toward a window to catch the light. I knew from experience that the inside of the old shotgun barrel was probably about as sooty as the inside of the stovepipe from the cook stove.

"You ever clean this thing?"

"No, not the inside," Uncle Jubal said, a bit defensively. "Sometimes I wipe off the outside of it with some of her sewing machine oil. I figure the inside of the barrel takes care of itself. It sorta cleans it every time I shoot it."

"This gun's been fired recently, real recently," the sheriff said. "Here, smell it," he said, offering it to one of the deputies to confirm.

"I shot a snake with it yesterday."

"We're taking the gun with us, back to town, maybe for evidence."

"Are y'all accusing me of killing Cutshaw?"

"No, at least not yet. Don't get upset. But we've got a job to do."

"When do I get my gun back?"

"When the law's through with it."

"What if I see another snake that needs shooting?"

"Kill it with a garden hoe, chop its head off."

There was no use arguing with the sheriff, we could see that, and after poking around in the outbuildings, they left with the gun.

"Stay all night, bo," Uncle Jubal said. "Them women are gone and I get lonesome."

I knew he'd make me cook.

We were both clumsy about it, but we managed. He brought out a fresh ham from his smokehouse and gave me a big butcher knife. I hacked and struggled and finally got two slices of the salt-cured pork freed from the ham. I could see the glaze glistening on the edges and we soaked it in a pan of water to try and get some of the salt out.

"It's good; always cure my own stuff," Uncle Jubal said, obviously relieved that the law was gone. "But if you don't soak it, we'll be up drinking water all night—gives you an awful thirst."

I fried the two ham slabs on the electric stove and also some thick-cut potatoes. It wasn't bad, and the biscuits Aunt Alma had made that morning were still good.

The phone rang about nine that evening. We could hear it from our rocking chairs on the porch. Uncle Jubal had been deep in a story from the War Between The States, something about all the battles in Virginia his grandfather had seen. I was enjoying it.

"Answer that thing, will you, Wes? I still ain't used to having that bell in the house all the time."

It was Aunt Alma, calling from Wilmington. The phone I was speaking on was part of a party line arrangement in which some folks listened in on all the conversations. There were probably eavesdroppers in the house in Wilmington, too. Plus the long-distance operator who'd placed the call for her. Maybe a dozen different people listening to every word we said. Aunt Alma knew it, too.

"We got here all right," she said, and I could tell she was talking slower than usual, making an effort to pronounce every word distinctly. "We'll be coming back tomorrow. Is everything all right there?"

"Yes, ma'am, we're fine. I cooked up some ham for supper, on the electric stove."

"You make sure you get it turned off, son, you hear me? I don't trust it. It might burn the house down."

"Yes, ma'am, I'll check it again before we go to bed."

"Tell Jubal everything is fine here." She continued to speak slowly, letting every word sink in. "Everything is very good here."

"I'll tell him. Thanks for calling us. See y'all tomorrow."

She said everything was fine, told me that two or three times. Uncle Jubal said that meant the gun was hidden now in an attic in Wilmington, in a relative's house who didn't even know that the gun was there.

"That relative," he said, "is an old maid aunt who lives alone and thinks Aunt Alma went up into the attic to look for an old picture frame or something. The gun'll never be found or seen again."

He launched back into his account of the war, which included an eyewitness description of the battle at Fredericksburg, given to him by his grandfather. I thought about modern war I had seen in the Pacific and went to sleep that night dreaming of musket fire and rebel yells.

Hillbilly had been fond of the rebel yell and could do it well, much better than my own feeble efforts. Before the raid on Makin, he had a saying about the Japs, something from the mountains, maybe from the old Cherokee days. He would use it from time to time when talking about the enemy and what we would do to them, the fierce tribal team talk that young warriors do. "Boys," he would say, "we'll knock their damn dick strings in the dirt."

I woke up thinking about the hillbilly from Murphy and his crazy highland sayings, glad he had survived. We found a scrap or two of the leftover ham and a cold biscuit apiece and called it breakfast.

Things calmed down then for about a week. Rumors flew around Carverville about Frog Cutshaw and who might have killed him, but even that subsided.

Then I got a call at the office from Caney Fork.

"Aunt Alma, is that you?"

"Honey, I've got bad news."

"Well, tell me . . . what is it?"

"The sheriff come and they took Jubal away, charged him with murdering that Frog Cutshaw. Son, what are we going to do?"

Twelve

UNCLE JUBAL HAD his own cell in the White County Jail, which was some sort of respect or recognition, I supposed. A jailer put me in there with him and left us to talk.

"I never thought it would come to this," Uncle Jubal said.

His voice was low because there were other prisoners in the next cell, but I could tell he was worried. Confident in his role in the Caney Fork execution, but surprised that he would actually be charged and jailed.

"They can't prove anything, no eyewitnesses."

"I know that, son, but it's embarrassing."

"We need to get you out of here."

"I'm gonna need a lawyer, too, to fight this thing. Will Herman take my case?"

"I'm sure he will. I'll ask him, and I'll check on your bond, see what it'll take to get you out. I'm not going to let them convict you—you and I both know you're innocent, and we both know who was there and pulled the trigger."

Uncle Jubal got teary-eyed and squeezed my hand. I thought to myself, *There's only one witness who could place me at the scene. I just hope the law never questions the vet's wife, June.*

UNCLE HERMAN sat in his big chair and looked across the desk hard at me, unasked questions in his eyes. "So Jubal Bailey wants me to defend him on a charge of murder?"

"Yes sir. He sent me to ask you."

"You're sort of in the middle, so to speak, on this aren't you, Wes?"

"Yes sir, I am. But he needs you."

"I asked you about your possible involvement the day of

the killing. You said you weren't a participant. You still say that?"

"Yes sir, I do." I hated to lie to my own uncle, but really, I think he preferred it that way. Just a hunch.

"Well, I'm going to take that as your final answer. And I'm not going to ask you any more about it. If it turns out that you were involved, even in a small way, I'd rather not know it. Of course I'll take the case," he said, grinning now. "I always like a good murder case and I can get him off clean and free. The district attorney's office has nothing but a circumstantial case against him, and I'll cut it to ribbons." I could see the fire in his eyes now, with the vision of a courtroom battle dancing in both our heads.

"We'll knock their dick strings in the dirt," I said, feeling combat coming on.

"What did you say?"

"Aw, it was just something I heard in the Marines."

"Sounds trashy, Wes, don't say it again. Some of the riffraff you served with may have influenced you in an undesirable way."

He instructed me on how to make bond for Uncle Jubal, called a judge and got the amount lowered to make it easier. That afternoon, I went to the magistrate's office in the jailhouse and, as a local property owner, put up the deed for my father's house as bond for Uncle Jubal. In ten minutes, he walked out of the jail to my waiting coupe and we were on the winding road to Caney Fork.

Aunt Alma cried and hugged him and kissed him. They didn't normally show this much emotion in front of me, but it was a family moment. She hugged me, too, and took us to the kitchen table.

"Uncle Herman is the best lawyer in White County," I assured them." He'll take care of you, and we'll win this thing in the courtroom."

"What do you reckon he'll charge us?" Aunt Alma asked.

"It don't matter, woman, we'll have to pay it."

"I know that, Jubal, just wondering if the boy knows how much Herman will charge."

I shook my head, no help there.

"We got some money in the bank," Uncle Jubal said. "And I know Herman takes land sometimes for pay. I've got a good farm here. We could slice off a few acres and not be hurt. Especially some of the lower end where we don't farm it."

"June was there that morning," I said, changing the subject. "Shooting at Frog with her husband's rifle. She never hit him, but she shot a bunch of times—maybe six or seven—and she saw me and ran away."

"That poor girl," Aunt Alma said, "what she's been through on account of that devil."

"The empty hulls, the brass from that Army rifle she was shooting, will still be on the ground there somewhere. We need the sheriff to come and see that, put it in as evidence. It'll muddy the water on their case."

"You're gonna make a good lawyer your ownself," Aunt Alma said.

My uncle nodded. "Get Willard to do it. He can tell the sheriff that he found the hulls and show exactly where. Didn't you tell me that Willard went over there to see Frog's body?"

"Yeah, he said half the community was over there, white and colored, tromping around and staring at the body."

"Well, Willard talks good and he's not involved. He can do it."

I drew a map on a piece of paper for Willard, telling them both as I drew exactly where and how it happened. Where June had been standing in thick honeysuckle, apparently hunkered down until Frog's truck came, then rising to shoot directly at him, and me.

"Tell Willard to look for the honeysuckle vines right across from the big pine. There should be bullet marks on the pine—she was dropping bark all over me. And something else, it took a while for all this to come back to me. She never hit Frog, but one of her bullets took out his windshield. There should be some glass maybe along the road. Anything Willard can find and make the deputies come and look at will weaken their case against you."

Uncle Jubal smiled and said he'd get Willard right on it.

A WEEK OR SO later, I got a full report from Willard himself. He came by the office in town but I preferred to talk outside, for obvious reasons.

We had never told anyone of Uncle Jubal's lapse at the critical moment—it would have been too shameful for him. He had thanked me later that morning, said he'ad never fainted in his whole life.

So Willard, and Aunt Alma as far as I know, and all the rest, figured that Uncle Jubal had burned Frog down with the pump gun. And it was funny, since I had actually done it, for me to be running around free and focusing on getting Uncle Jubal found innocent. And by working hard on his defense, I could really forget from time to time who had actually pulled the trigger.

"I had to pester the damn sheriff for a day or two to get him to send out a deputy," Willard said. The youngest of their brood, he wasn't quite as religious as Uncle Jubal and used stronger language from time to time.

"He was kin to Frog, you know, and I really reckon he thinks he's got the case agin Jubal all tied up. But I kept after him, come to see him twice and then called on the phone. Had to go to the neighbor's to make the call—we ain't got a phone yet."

"But you got a good car," I said, winking at him. "Made two trips to Wilmington and back."

"Yeah, my woman's a good driver."

"What did you find? Did you use that little map I drew for you?" I asked.

"Y'r map was all right, but it took some doing to find exactly where she was standing. I went out there and looked and poked around a long time 'fore I found anything."

Willard said he got hot with the sheriff on the phone and the officer finally agreed to send a deputy the following morning. They met at the scene and Willard led him to the evidence.

"I told him 'Hellfire, y'all got my brother charged with a

killing here he never done. You better get this and take a strong look at it.' I showed him the rifle hulls, found four of them in the honeysuckle, and there was some pieces of glass in the road but not much. Most of the glass stayed in the truck. I recollect seeing it when I come to see Frog that morning. It was on the seat in the truck. In fact, some of it was still a-laying on the hood.

"That deputy took them four brass hulls and put them in a little paper poke like you'd get candy in at a store. Then he took another little poke out and put the glass in it. He wrote something on the outside of the pokes, like the date or something, and then he put the both of them inside a big paper sack like you'd get groceries in and wrote a date or something on it. Real careful man."

"Willard, what do the people on Caney Fork think about it?" I asked.

"Some of 'em think Jubal might have done it, most don't care a lot and they all talk about it all the time. Some think maybe the rogues that sold him the t'ars mighta done it.

"The colored boy that worked for him, named Reuben, disappeared, you know, about that time and that's causing a lot of talk. I even heered it mighta been somebody from ten years back that he cheated outa some money when he was hauling whiskey, an old debt that caught up with him."

"That's a new one on me, but repeat it all you can."

"Oh, I am. Me and the wife, we try to spread it as much as we can. Tell everybody that ol' Jubal never done it."

I reported to Uncle Herman about the rifle brass and the shards of windshield glass now in the sheriff's hands. He probably knew about it quicker than the district attorney did.

"Good work," he said. "We'll call for that at trial. Confuse the jury with evidence that there was a second shooter. Good work." And he wrote down Willard's name as a defense witness.

My education as a would-be lawyer went on constantly, and if I had a question about something, he would usually take time to lecture to me. He often spoke in legal language, which always caught my ear.

"This is the first time I've been this close to a murder trial,."

I said. "I keep wondering . . . how do you defend a man you know is guilty?"

"Hell, Wes, as you've probably noticed, I haven't asked Jubal of his guilt and I haven't pressed you on your own possible involvement in this matter. I don't want to know anymore than I already know. However, in my various and sundry roles as counselor, I must take the high road always and maintain and uphold the legal system. Even if I know a man to be guilty as sin, I would still represent him to the best of my abilities."

"Why, even if he was a bad actor and you knew he deserved punishing?"

"Son, if he deserves punishment, he'll probably get it. Regardless of my sterling defense of him, he'll get it. I look at it this way. The law is a strange and a wonderful thing and I have committed my life to it. The law says that if a man is accused, he deserves a chance to confront his accusers and the witnesses against him. And he deserves to have legal counsel to represent him. That's what I do.

"The poor devil standing in front of the court feels like the whole world is against him, and often it is. He deserves to have a spokesman to speak for him, someone who knows how the game is played."

"So it's a game?"

"Not exactly, but you understand what I'm saying. The prosecutor and his boys will do certain things to hammer their case home for the jury, and the defense will do certain things to counter and to try to win. And to win sometimes means just to get your man less time on the chain gang."

"How about Uncle Jubal . . . will he get the death penalty or the chain gang?"

"Hopefully, neither one. I think we can beat it completely and he can walk out a free man. So far, their case is weak, but they have one damaging piece of evidence."

"What is that?"

"One of the sheriff's deputies went to Raleigh for a special law enforcement school last year and he's pretty good. He made a cast out of some sort of white plaster and they'll have it in court.

"You know your uncle wears a distinctive thick-soled shoe on one side and sorta drags his foot when he walks. They've got a cast of one of Jubal's tracks, which they said was within ten feet of the body."

TURKEY JACK TOOK me down into South Carolina about the middle of October, to look at a sawmill he wanted to buy. "I heard about this through the grapevine, you know how people talk. It might be a good deal, and it might not. We'll just have to go and look.

"She wants to go, too. Her people live down there and she ain't seen any of them in a long time."

It took me a moment to figure out that his Geechee woman would be making the trip with us.

"We'll have to take the truck, may be going back in the woods a-ways to see this rig."

Which is how I found myself jammed into the cab of a truck with Turkey Jack Lowery, the Geechee woman and a big sack of clothing.

"She's taking some clothes to her sister," Jack said. "Sorry, but with this rain falling, we cain't put the sack in the back or it'll get wet."

Jack and the Geechee woman each had an odor about them, a mixture of wood smoke from the shack they lived in, and body sweat.

It was a rank scent that I'd never noticed much before because I'd been near them only outside. Here, cooped up in a truck cab for two hours with them, the smell of the fresh rain coming in through a partly-open window was delightful.

"This mill we gonna look at is supposed to be down by Georgetown," Jack said. "We'll drop her off with her people, go look at it, and then come back and get her."

The woman never spoke—she apparently only conversed with Jack.

"This old man had the mill and he's died out. His widow owns it now, and I hear she'll sell it right. It ain't been run in about a year—we'll have to see what shape it's in."

"What kind of price is she wanting?"

"Don't know that. We'll try to jew her down on the price. Hate to take advantage of a widow woman, but if we don't, somebody else will."

"How'd you hear about this deal?"

"At the lumber company where we're selling our logs all the time. One of the fellows there's got a cousin down here. Got the word that way."

An hour later, Jack drove the logging truck into a cluster of unpainted shacks in a briar patch near Georgetown. The big dual wheels on the rear sent water flying from puddles in the dirt road, and colored children ran out from the houses onto flimsy porches to get a better look at us.

"Here we go, this is it," Jack said. "They'll put you to work, girl." A group of women were gathered on the open porch of this particular house, doing something with their hands which seemed to be manipulating straw.

"What are they doing, Jack?"

"I can answer that for him, Jack. Let me tell it." The Geechee woman had spoken, in a low throaty voice. It was the first time I had really ever heard her say anything. It was amazing. "The women of the Sea Islands, my people, who are called Gullah or Geechee, make baskets from grass and pine needles. It's a craft they brought with them from Mother Africa."

I was fascinated at the musical rhythm of her voice. Her words gave evidence of education, not the slurred slang of a field worker. And she looked directly at me with a sense of pride and dignity I had never seen in a colored woman.

"Young Wes, the apple of my Jack's eye, come with me and let me show you," she said, shoving me out the truck door into the drizzling rain. Flabbergasted at the torrent of words from her mouth, I followed her onto the porch. I looked back once at Turkey Jack and he seemed slightly embarrassed.

"Ladies, this visitor wishes to see how the baskets are made. Kindly show him the stages of completion of your work.

Perhaps he will buy."

They were giggling at me now, a classic scene of females outnumbering the male and amused at his predicament. I was shown the base of a basket in one set of ebony hands, and a half-finished one, then taken inside the house where dozens were stacked on the floor.

"My name is Felicia," Jack's woman said, extending her hand. "Please don't ever think of me as just another Geechee woman again. Or as Jack's woman, although I'm sure there've been others before me. I am my *own* person."

The other women beamed and I shook hands with her. "Pick out three of the baskets," I told her, "for my aunts and my girlfriend. I will pay for them when we come back to get you."

She smiled and said, "We'll have lots to talk about on the way home."

"Jack, where in the world did you get her?"

"It's a long story, bo, I'm sure she'll tell you all about it on the way home." He looked a little henpecked, like even speaking about Felicia was dangerous.

We found the mill owner half an hour later, after asking directions in town. Some of the sawmill had been dismantled and was in her barn safe from the weather. Some of it was still at the last site where it had been used prior to her husband's death. A sturdy lady, she climbed up into the truck with us and guided us to it.

"He run it with two men to help him. We were just a small operation," the woman said. "But it made purty good money and he liked working outdoors. Y'all are loggers, you know the life."

"Yes ma'am," Turkey Jack said. "We just want to be able to go another step up with it. 'Stead of selling our raw logs to a mill, we could cut it and plane it and get a better price."

Out here in the woods, the small mill was open to the air but at least there was a tin-roofed shed above it. The big circular blade had a film of surface rust. Jack wiped at it with his finger and said the first log that went through it would polish the rust off.

"Can we have the shed and the tin, too?" he asked.

She said, "If you'll tear it down yourself, it goes with the deal."

Jack said, "We can shore do that, if we can agree on a price."

Basically, she had three pieces of equipment to offer: the saw itself, an old planer and a gas engine that was the power unit to run the planer and the saw, which it did through a series of heavy belts.

She wanted twelve hundred dollars but Jack told her we were just poor loggers. We couldn't pay that much. He had told me on the trip down that a thousand dollars would be a fair price and a good buy. He started the bidding at eight hundred. She twisted her lips and came down to a thousand.

"Me and Wes came today ready to buy, ma'am," Jack said solemnly, "but we cain't jump quite that high. We'll give you nine hundred dollars, cash money, and we'll take the planer today. Come back next week when it quits raining and get the rest of the stuff."

"I got another man supposed to be coming tomorrow to look at it," she said, looking off into the distance and seemingly talking to herself, "but a bird in the hand is worth more than one off in the bushes somewhere. Let me see your money, it's a deal."

We went back to town, hired two draft dodgers we found at the local pool hall to help us, and backed up to her barn to load the heavy planer. We found a block and tackle in the barn, and with a lot of groaning and grunting got the old planer on the truck and covered it with a tarp for the ride home.

"Looks like you have a locomotive on the back of your truck," Felicia said.

"It's about the same size and weighs about the same," Jack told her. "Get in, and let's ride."

"First, let Wes pay for his baskets."

I approved her selections and paid the colored women on the porch for three seagrass baskets, with intricate designs of alternating light and dark stripes.

"I was born down near Charleston, on what used to be an

old rice plantation," Felicia began. And despite her wonderful musical voice, it was a long story and I almost fell asleep. The labor of loading the planer and the steady drum of the rain on the truck's metal roof made me drowsy. Turkey Jack, the legendary wild man of the swamp, looked even more henpecked as his woman took and held center stage.

Night fell and we drove on, slowed by the heavy load on the truck. Felicia told in detail how the white plantation owners had been thrilled by the sound of her voice and paid for her to go to New York City and study music. She told of voice lessons with opera people and also of singing in Harlem jazz clubs, dropping famous names that I had barely heard of.

"But I got lonesome for home," she said, "and came back to the Carolina coast and started hearing stories about Turkey Jack Lowery. Equal parts red, black and white, and all man. They told me stories about him until I was determined to meet him." She laughed and patted Jack on the cheek. He looked embarrassed and pulled his head away. "So I moved into a dump on the edge of a swamp to keep house for my Jack. He keeps me safe and he makes me happy."

We entered Carverville on the side of town where the courthouse and the jail are, Jack slowly gaining block by block with the old Chicago planer looming high on the truck bed—our planer now. In a week or so, we'd have a whole sawmill that would be ours.

He made the turn at the jail street and the headlights revealed a strange scene. Two deputies were escorting a woman in a light-colored dress, no hat or coat to protect her from the rain, her hands clenched together at her waist and the sheen of the shiny handcuffs binding them glistening in the light drizzle.

She jerked her face toward the sound of the groaning truck motor and I sat straight up in my seat. It was the dead vet's wife, June.

And suddenly I wasn't sleepy any more.

Thirteen

"JUBAL MADE A speech, didn't he? Sometime back, he made a speech at the store against Cutshaw?" Uncle Herman cross-examined me across his big mahogany desk. "Answer son, tell me."

"So that's the way you do it . . . looking hard, right in the eyes and boring in with your questions."

"Pay attention, Wes," he said, but he was grinning now and enjoying the teacher-pupil situation. "You're beginning to learn, and when we get in the courtroom, it'll go real fast." He took on his formal role again and his deep courtroom voice. "The witness will please answer the question."

"Yes sir, he did make a speech."

"And it was public, at the Cutshaw store, in front of witnesses?"

"I believe that is correct, sir."

"And in that public utterance, Jubal Bailey did say in his own words that Cutshaw should be killed, that his death would make Caney Fork a better place to live, or something like that?"

"Yes sir, he did."

"You weren't actually there that day, were you, Wes?" Softening now, he became the uncle instead of the prosecutor.

"No, sir," I told him, "but Uncle Jubal told me about it and Willard did, too. It was right after Frog and some others tried to do an abortion—is that what you call it?—on that girl.

"They dug up inside her with a rusty piece of wire and she swelled up and died. Uncle Jubal and everybody else was mad as the devil about it. That's when he said that to Frog's face, for everybody to hear."

Uncle Herman nodded. "Well, the district attorney's office knows all about it and they'll have witnesses to testify that Jubal said it. The prosecution will portray it to the jury as a threat, a death threat said in public by the defendant.

"They've got that, they've got his gun which was fired in a time-frame that fits the killing and they've got his track at the scene. Plus the fact that Jubal was a neighbor of Frog's hog lot, so to speak, whether he liked it or not. So proximity is going to figure in this. The prosecution will probably draw a map and show that Jubal's farm and Cutshaw's land joined at the creek and Jubal was probably the closest man to Cutshaw when Cutshaw was killed."

He looked glum then, mentally figuring the odds against him. But I had infinite faith in Uncle Herman—he didn't lose many cases in White County.

"Don't worry, Uncle Herman, we'll knock their dick strings in the dirt."

"I told you not to use that expression, son, it sounds like some of the white trash slang from your Marine days."

"Well, you'll win. I know you will."

"I hope you're right. White County hasn't had a death penalty case in three years and I wasn't in on the last one. This district attorney we've got now was, though, and he was a bulldog in that one. Went right at it and won, sent the man to the gas chamber."

"Was he guilty?"

"Oh yeah, guilty as sin. But the point is that the defense in that case could have done better than they did. And the district attorney didn't show any slack, no mercy at all. Went for it and he got it. He can preach just like an old-timey tent revival for a country jury."

"Don't sell yourself short, Uncle, you're good, too. They talk about you around the courthouse and the way you can speak when you get wound up."

"Well, you better get over to the clerk's office and see your sweet little Darlene and get us a copy of the jury pool. I hear the clerk finally got the names last week, and drew an extra hundred just in case we need them for this murder case.

"And when you get the names, you and Darlene need to

plan on going through the court records together. It's public information—they can't stop you. I'm going to want to know which jurors have court records, if they've ever been in court themselves. And ask if Darlene, or any of the other women in that office, know if these jurors are related to anyone who has been in court."

I could see his logic, the preparation shaping up. Picking the jury would be a battle, most of it unseen facts that would guide Uncle Herman to accept this one or reject that one. And a lifetime of living in White County would be helpful, too.

"Bring me the names first, let me look at them. I'll know a lot of them personally and Hilda will know some of them, too. Then you and Darlene can go into the criminal records with the list."

I was almost out the door when he called me back and looked directly at me again. He could make me feel uncomfortable, like he was looking right into my heart. But I could stand it.

"One more thing, Wes. It's dangerous and I know the district attorney will play this up when we get to trial."

"What's that?"

"Whoever killed Mr. Frog Cutshaw that morning out at Caney Fork didn't rob the man."

"So . . . what does that mean?"

"They didn't rob the man. They left the body lying there and deputies found a roll of money in his pants pocket, nearly a thousand dollars.

"I have heard the loose talk around the town, same as you have heard. But if a bootlegger from his past had caught up with Cutshaw, especially if he was killed for an old debt, they would have surely robbed him. Secondly, if the missing colored boy had shot him, then he would certainly have robbed him." He slipped into debate style. "And thirdly, if the black-market tire people had assassinated him, they would have robbed him and probably would have done it at the store, most likely never knew about his hog lot routine."

I didn't reply but I was mentally kicking myself for not

taking Frog's money that morning. It had never crossed my mind, we were in such a hurry to get out of there.

"The killing of Frog Cutshaw was a crime of extreme passion, Wes, and the district attorney will make much of that fact. Whoever killed the man deeply hated him."

"Maybe not," I told him, "maybe they intended to rob him but were frightened away by someone coming. Things are not always as they seem." It was an original thought. I was very proud of it.

Uncle Herman said, "I'll have to think about that."

"HERE'S YOUR LIST," Darlene said, leaning across the counter at the Clerk of Court's office. "And here's a kiss." Nobody else was around and she offered her lips for a long, slow kiss. Then held up her left hand for me to admire the diamond for the umpteenth time.

"I can't believe we're engaged. Ever since you gave it to me at Christmas, I've had trouble sleeping at night, I'm so happy."

"You'll have trouble when you start sleeping with me, too."

"Oh, hush, there'll be plenty of time for that later."

"Have you got all your wedding plans made? It's just two more months until June."

"Silly, of course I have. But I'm worried about your colored lady singer."

Concern now showed in her pretty face, so I had to kiss her again. "Don't worry about Felicia. She trained in New York City, and sings like an opera star. She'll be great."

"Okay," she said, "here's the jury list."

I reminded her that Uncle Herman was paying her for after-hours work and there would be a meeting tonight at his office. "I'll pick you up about seven."

"That's fine."

"HERE'S THE LIST," Uncle Herman told us that night, meeting in the big room where conference sessions were held between the firm's lawyers and their clients. Herman had me and

Darlene, but he also had two good sources of background material. One was the town water meter reader, the other a rural mail carrier. Both good strong Democrats and between them, they knew about everybody in the town and the county.

"Religion is very important in this case," Herman told us. "I'm going to question every potential juror on their denomination, and their religious practices. Jubal Bailey is a God-fearing man and jurors of like mind will empathize with him. I want to know their legal troubles, if they've been in court as a defendant. If so, they may distrust the sheriff's department and I want to exploit that feeling if their children have been in trouble with the law.

"And I want to know their relatives, if any of them are kin to a policeman somewhere or a deputy. Would they have a natural tendency to side with the law because of a brother or cousin?"

Darlene and I worked steadily three afternoons late at the clerk's office, digging into court records and looking at files. A man doing similar work glanced at us from time to time but never said anything. Darlene said he was from the district attorney's office and seemed to be doing the same thing we were.

"He knows nothing about the meter reader and the mailman," I told her. "And Uncle Herman on his own knows about half the people in the county. We're in good shape."

THE TRIAL STARTED the second week of April, 1944, as the second week of a two-week special term of Superior Court. The first week was taken up with quickie criminal cases in which the defendants pled guilty and got their sentences. Uncle Herman had a dozen of these and was constantly at the courthouse the first two days of that week.

Then they had three days set aside for civil lawsuit cases and he thought the disputed will case from the Cape Fear end of the county would come up, but one of the lawyers on the other side was sick and it got continued.

Uncle Herman shook his head. "We'll be on the hot spot next week, Wes. It'll take all day Monday to pick a jury, and then the DA will start in with his stuff on Tuesday. May take all week. Tell Jubal and Alma to dress in their Sunday best and keep smiling."

Monday morning jury selection began, with me sitting at the defense table between my two uncles. Jubal was plainly nervous but confident in his defense team. Herman was just as plainly enjoying the verbal combat to come. Aunt Alma sat on the front row in the courtroom, right behind Uncle Jubal, separated only by the railing that divided the room. She was beaming, a happy optimistic person who lit up the place with her personality. You'd never know by looking that her husband was on trial for his life.

Our notes on the jurors were in a ragged pile, held together by a rubber band. Uncle Herman would check on them occasionally, but most of the time, he knew his stuff without looking. There were six men on the list who had had trouble with the law in the past and could reasonably be expected to vote against the sheriff if given the chance.

There was one old man the meter reader said was a Holiness deacon at a Holy Roller church on the edge of Carverville. Herman said he would identify strongly with Uncle Jubal and we wanted him on the panel badly.

There were several women, too, which Uncle Herman said could be trouble. One especially, who was reputed to have a brother who was a policeman in another town. She had also worked a year prior at a military base in Virginia, and was said to be a strong-talking woman. "We don't need no uppity women on this jury—just takes one to foul things up," Herman said. "We'll set her down if they don't."

The DA, it soon was apparent, had little use for women jurors at all and sent them all home. Uncle Herman questioned the remaining jurors closely on religious preferences and soon all proved to be Baptist, with a Methodist or two thrown in.

"You heard the joke about Baptists and Methodists," Herman told us at a break in the proceedings. "A Methodist is just a Baptist that's learned to read and write."

Uncle Jubal, who was a Baptist, laughed politely but shook his head.

"Hilda was raised a Methodist," Herman said. "I always use that one on her."

Ten minutes later, he dismissed a juror who seemed satisfactory to me.

"He's Episcopalian," he whispered for explanation.

"You cull a man for being Episcopalian?"

"Yeah," he whispered, "most Episcopalians are high-class folks. Might take the law too seriously, vote the wrong way. Don't need them on my jury."

"Is there any reason you couldn't serve a week, if needed, on this case?" the DA asked a man, who was straining forward to hear the question.

"No, I don't believe I know him." Laughter.

"Sir, do you hear well?"

"Yes sir, I live near here." More laughter.

"Your honor, this juror is plainly not competent. Request dismissal by the bench," the DA said.

The judge nodded and a bailiff escorted the man out of the room, past the smirking crowd. The judge was from Charlotte, Herman said, an unknown quantity who had never held court in Eastern Carolina before.

"We don't know how to read this one," Herman said, "he kept to himself pretty much the first week and he showed us that he runs a tight ship. His court runs on time, four hours in the morning, four hours in the afternoon. I don't think he drinks anything at all."

"That dang old judge kept us in there almost till six o'clock," I told Darlene that night. "We got twelve picked, and one alternate, all men. Herman's pleased."

"Who got picked of all those we researched? Did it help any?"

"Some. The DA was sharp, too, and all the men who had troubles with the Law got thrown off. But we got two men on there whose sons have been in court—the DA must not know about them. And that old Holiness deacon is sitting right on the front row in the jury box. He'll like Jubal. He's a good one for us."

"The clerk's letting me work in the courtroom tomorrow, not much to do really but keep watch on the jury. I'll get to see everything this week."

Uncle Jubal's murder trial had drawn a full room, even for the jury picking. Tomorrow promised to be standing room only. A big trial was big doings in Carverville.

Fourteen

"THEY'VE CHANGED it around a little," Herman said Tuesday morning. "Normally, the sheriff would be their lead-off witness, but he's going to be second. The DA will start with their smart-ass deputy."

The chief deputy, who had the special training in Raleigh and had made the plaster cast of Uncle Jubal's track, took the oath and began to testify.

Prompted by questions from the stem DA, obviously well-rehearsed, he told how he and other officers had been summoned to Caney Fork and found Frog Cutshaw dead beside his hog lot.

"There was no need to call for a doctor then, the man was dead?" the DA asked.

"Yes sir, stone cold, four-o'clock dead."

"Could you determine the cause of death?"

"The coroner did that, sir, but it was plain to me that he had been hit several times with buckshot. Shot in the face and the chest."

"Did you find shell casings at the scene?"

"Yes sir, we sure did. Three of them We've got them there on the table in a paper bag."

"Tell us about the tracks you saw there . . . and your special training in reading tracks."

"I attended a school last year in Raleigh for law officers. They taught us a lot about tracks and other scientific things. I looked in the mud and saw a bunch of tracks, but one caught my eye."

"Go on, tell us about it, please."

"There was one peculiar track, looked like the man dragged

his foot when he walked and the shape of the sole was different from all the others. I found a good one in some fresh mud and made a cast from it. It's there on the table, too."

"Did you identify who made the track?"

"Yes sir, we did. We compared it to some tracks in his yard and he let us look at his shoe. He's got one leg shorter than the other and he has to wear a special shoe on one foot. It belongs to the man sitting there at the defense table, Mr. Jubal Bailey."

"Let the record show that the witness has identified the defendant as the maker of the track. Your witness, counselor." The DA almost snarled the last, looking at Uncle Herman with a smirk. This DA was scary.

"Deputy, you've been off to a school and got educated, haven't you?" Uncle Herman started off in high gear, poking a little fun at the officer. "You know how to make casts of tracks, do stuff the other pore old deputies cain't do, don't you?"

I looked deliberately at the two jurors whose sons had been before a judge in this very room and they were smiling at the officer's discomfort.

"Deputy, we're not going to deny that Jubal Bailey was at that murder scene," Herman said, the volume of his voice rising and his words taking on a rhythm of their own. I was beginning to hear the orator. "Mr. Officer, the defendant Jubal Bailey had every right to visit that murder scene like everybody else in Caney Fork did, and he went there to see for himself the bloody body. He's gonna testify that he went there in broad daylight, makes no secret of it, but he was an innocent bystander and not a perpetrator."

"Objection," the DA said. "Objection, the defense lawyer is brazenly testifying himself."

"Sustained," the judge said. "Defense will kindly refrain from offering testimony."

"Yes, sir. Sorry, sir. I was merely summarizing evidence that will be given in due time from the witness chair by the defendant.

"Now, sir," he said, staring hard at the deputy. "You've got a track but you don't know exactly when it was made, do you?"

"No, sir, but I would say sometime that morning. It was fresh."

"We know it was fresh, we'll gladly admit that. If Jubal Bailey, a God-fearing Baptist deacon from Caney Fork, wants to go to a murder scene and look it over, is it logical to assume that he would leave a track there?"

"Yes, sir, it is."

"How many folks were at the scene that morning when you and your fellow officers arrived?"

"I'd say twenty-five or thirty, sir."

"White and colored?"

"Yes, both white and colored."

"Every one of them stomping around the body and the truck, looking and poking and tracking up the place. Is that correct?"

"Yes, sir ."

"Now, tell me this. You found some shotgun shells in the mud out there?"

"Yes sir, found three. There on the table."

"That'll be all," Uncle Herman said, "but as sort of an expert here, we may want to call you back at a future time." The DA nodded agreement and the first witness stepped down.

The sheriff was next and they got Uncle Jubal's old single-shot gun into evidence real quick. The sheriff said it had been fired recently, about the time of the killing, and the DA waved the gun around as much as he could in front of the jury, then placed it on the witness table in plain view.

"Sheriff, is this a 12 gauge gun?" the DA asked.

"Yes, sir, it is. Same size gun as the shells we found at the hog lot beside the dead man."

"Sheriff, did the defendant give any explanation?"

"He said he had shot the gun at a snake or a crow or something. I don't remember exactly why he said it had been fired."

"Sheriff, how fast can a man shoot and reload this kind of gun?"

"Pretty fast. Most of these old farmers keep this kind of gun around and they do shoot at crows and rabbits and such. They get used to it and they can handle them guns pretty fast."

"I want the jury to remember what he's saying now. You'll hear more on this, I'm sure. Your witness."

Uncle Herman had nothing but contempt for their case and it showed—he meant for it to show—in his cross-examination of the sheriff.

"The dead man was a relative of yours, was he not, Mr. Sheriff?"

"Yes sir, he was a cousin of mine."

"So you were angry about his murder and determined to find the guilty party, is that correct?"

"Yes, sir, and I believe we did just that."

"Come on now, Sheriff, you arrested a man but you've got a mighty flimsy case against him, haven't you?"

"I wouldn't say exactly that . . ."

"You've got a track that you say is his and you don't know when it was made. You got an old shotgun that has been fired, but you don't know when, or under what circumstances, now do you?"

The sheriff didn't want to answer at all, but Herman pressed him and he finally said no, real low. Then he was dismissed.

The DA put on two witnesses, local Caney Fork folks that had heard Uncle Jubal's speech at the store, saying that the community would be a better place if Frog Cutshaw was dead. Uncle Herman declined to question either one, letting their stories pass without comment.

Then a deputy sheriff brought June to the prosecution table and my heart skipped a beat or two. What would she say, the one person who could place me at the scene moments before Frog Cutshaw's mean life ended? Uncle Jubal looked at me and grimaced. Herman didn't know what was possible now.

The DA established that she was a resident of the neighborhood where the store was located, living near Jubal Bailey and the Cutshaw store. But after that, he lost control and it was obvious he wasn't sure why his team had called June.

When he stopped for a breath, she burst out loudly, "I said out loud in a café right here in Carverville that I was glad Frog was dead and deputies brought me in, in handcuffs fer saying it. I didn't appreciate that one little bit."

"Is it common knowledge in Caney Fork that Jubal Bailey said Frog needed to be dead?"

"Objection," Uncle Herman said.

"Go ahead," the judge said. "The witness can answer the question if she knows."

"Sure," June said. "Everybody knowed that. Mr. Jubal made a speech and said it for everybody to hear. The Baileys were enemies of Frog. Frog talked about it all the time. He hated 'em.

"I knew that girl that swoll up and died, she cried like a baby before she went."

"Where were you on the morning that Mr. Cutshaw died?" the DA asked, fishing for information that might help his case. Jubal and I both held our breath—this was it.

"In my house," June said, never missing a beat. "I never knowed nothing about it 'til some friends came by in an A-Model Ford and we drove down there, so I could see him dead with my own eyes. He killed my husband and I'm glad he's dead."

"That's enough," the DA said.

"Let her talk," Herman said.

The judge glared at both the DA and Uncle Herman and nodded to June to continue.

"He run over my husband like a dog in the road with that big fertilizer truck of his, squashed him like a bug. Law never done nothing about it, never even charged him with nothing."

The DA shook his head in frustration and passed her on to Herman to pose the next question.

"What's the general reputation of Jubal Bailey in the Caney Fork community, do you know?"

"He's a good man . . . a man of God, deacon in the church. He and his brothers and Wes there, they all come and fixed up our house for us before Frog killed my husband."

Uncle Herman said, "Fine, step down please," and in a soft

voice thanked the DA for that fine witness. His sarcasm wasn't wasted. I saw the judge grin a little at the taunt.

We recessed for lunch then, and every restaurant and café in Carverville was full. It was Big Court Week in earnest and all the spectators and jurors and lawyers crammed into the booths and crowded around the tables. Waitresses got tips and the cash registers rang.

Darlene and I and Uncle Herman ended up eating down at the café by the railroad and we saw the judge himself in there, by himself at a table in the corner.

Darlene held my hand as we walked back the two blocks to the courthouse for the afternoon session.

"Something happened back there," she said, under the shade of the trees on Main Street. "I don't understand, but she said to give this to you."

Uncle Herman had stayed behind at the café, talking to another lawyer about the Cape Fear will case. I was glad he wasn't around after I took the note and read it.

It was from June. She had given it to Darlene in the ladies room at the café. Written on a scrap of notebook paper in pencil, it said simply "I thank all of you for what you did for me. June." I crumpled it up and put it in my pocket.

"Wes, what's that mean? Who is that woman?"

"Just somebody Uncle Jubal and I helped out last year."

She raised her eyebrows at that but asked no more questions and began to talk about the wedding.

When the court cranked back up that afternoon, we went into chambers with the judge immediately on the rifle casings. Uncle Herman told the DA, "If you're not going to enter them into evidence, I am."

The DA said the rifle shells hadn't been seen by his office as evidence yet, but they did have possession of them.

"Our first witness tomorrow morning is going to be the defendant's brother Willard, who found them," Herman said. "We want that bag of shell casings to show to the jury."

"I don't have them," the DA said, "and I don't see why they need to come into this case since there's not a shred of evidence that they belong."

Uncle Herman said something then about getting the judge to issue a bench warrant, if that was necessary, to produce the evidence that the DA's office was withholding.

The judge looked pained and sent out for some stomach mints. He asked Uncle Herman if he had ever tried the chicken liver casserole down at the café, and told the DA to let Herman have the shell casings. "Let's get on with it," he said.

Back in the courtroom, the DA called another deputy sheriff, an older man who had investigated the shooting scene that day. He had also been at the doctor's office when a local doctor examined the body.

"What did the doctor find? What did you see with your own eyes removed from the dead body of Frog Cutshaw?" the DA asked.

"He took out several large lead balls—buckshot—from the man. One or two fell out on the ground when we loaded him up out at Caney Fork. And the doctor dug out seventeen more."

"Did you save the buckshot?"

"Yes sir, here it all is."

"I want the men of the jury to look at this, as I spread these bloody buckshot on the table. This is what took the life of Frog Cutshaw."

I filed that dramatic moment away for future reference.

The DA glared at Herman and enjoyed his moment. But he wasn't finished. "Before you step down, deputy, tell us, did you search the body?"

"Yes, sir, we sure did."

"And tell us what you found."

"He had that nickel-plated .45 in his right hand."

"Had it been fired?"

"It had. We had to be real careful taking it out of his hand 'cause it was loaded and cocked. Turned out it had been fired about three times, judging from the live bullets left in the clip."

"So you would say Frog Cutshaw was fighting for his life?"

"I reckon. Anyways, he was shooting his pistol when he died."

"And did you search his clothing?"

"Yeah, we did. Found a pocketknife, a pocket watch and nearly a thousand dollars in paper money."

"Tell the jury that again, please."

"We found nearly a thousand dollars in a roll in Mr. Cutshaw's pocket, paper money with a rubber band around it."

"So whoever killed Frog Cutshaw didn't rob him?"

"No, sir, the money was right there."

"Thank you, deputy. Your witness, Defense." The DA was smiling in triumph, the judge looked pale and grim. I saw him eat another stomach mint. Herman saw it, too.

So Uncle Herman played the part of the genial host and motioned for a conference at the bench. I tagged along, as did the DA's three assistants, for the conversation that wouldn't be heard by the jurymen.

"You're obviously in some discomfort, Your Honor," Herman said, "and there's really no reason to be in session the rest of this afternoon. I suggest that we adjourn for the remainder of the day, let this fine judge go to his room and heal, and the Defense will be ready to start first thing tomorrow morning.

"You're about done, aren't you?" he said to the DA, who nodded, but said he'd reserve the right to call any more witnesses for the prosecution if needed.

The judge thanked Herman for his motion to adjourn and it was done. I couldn't tell yet if we were winning, but the chicken liver casserole had apparently beaten the judge.

WEDNESDAY MORNING, Uncle Herman put Ruby on the stand first to establish where Uncle Jubal had been that morning. Herman said this was good. "We could have put your aunt on and she could have said he was with her at the time. But it's better to tell the jury that he was working that morning as a farmer and where he was at work."

He approached her. "Ruby, you and your children were pulling corn for Jubal Bailey, is that correct?"

"Yes, suh, it is. He had put a wagon in the cornfield and we wuz putting the corn in it."

"Your children were there too, they help you in the fields?"

"Yas, suh, in the fields and in ow-wah ga'den." The word our had two syllables but absolutely no "r", quite interesting.

Ruby said she had heard a lot of shooting from across the creek, on the Cutshaw land, but Mr. Jubal Bailey hadn't left the field and was with them working there all morning.

"How many children do you have?" the DA asked, moving quickly to discredit her. "Five."

"And who is the father of these five kids?"

Pressed hard and embarrassed, she admitted that they were fathered by three different men who were all long gone.

"I wish she'd get another man. I need somebody besides a woman and children to help me," Uncle Jubal whispered. Even at his own murder trial, the problem of keeping a good tenant family was hard on his mind. Finally, the DA let poor Ruby go.

We put Willard on next, who promptly identified himself as brother to the defendant, told about going to the scene after Jubal had been charged and finding the empties.

"There was a lot of windshield glass inside the cab of his truck and we all saw it," Willard said. "There was at least two different people shooting at him that morning and neither one of them was my oldest brother. Y'all ought to let him go."

Herman entered the rifle casings then as evidence, over the objections of the DA, who ripped into Willard on cross-examination. But he got as good as he gave.

"Sir, we are to believe that these cartridge hulls are somehow involved in this murder?"

"Yes sir, I found them at the place and got a deputy out there and showed him. Me and him picked 'em up and there they are on the table right now."

"Tell this court the truth. You don't know when these shells were fired, do you?"

"No sir, I truly don't; no more than you know when them shotgun hulls there was fired, or what kind of gun fired them." Some of the jurymen smirked on that reply and I felt good about it. The DA let him step down and Herman rose to call the well-schooled deputy back.

"Look at these empties, sir. Since you have gone to special law enforcement schooling, tell me what kind of gun fired them."

"It's some sort of military round; the Army's got a new gun they're using in the war, a little .30 caliber carbine, and that's it."

"A soldier's gun? That's what you're telling us."

"Yes sir, that's what it appears to be."

"Your Honor," Herman said, facing the jury and speaking at full volume now for effect. "I wish to make a motion at this time for the court to drop all charges against my client, on the grounds that a soldier may have been shooting at the deceased on that morning and my client wasn't there at all. There are too many variables in this case and I don't like any of them: a dead man full of holes, a military gun. Let Jubal Bailey go back to his farm."

The DA jumped to his feet to protest and the judge shook his head. Uncle Herman was good. He wouldn't get the motion he asked for, and in fact didn't expect to, but he was cutting the prosecution deeply with every word. And the jury was plainly enjoying the commotion, staged for its benefit, even elbowing each other in the ribs and pointing so as not to miss any of the action. For dramatic effect, Uncle Herman seized the handful of carbine hulls with a nice flourish and offered them to the judge. "Look," he almost shouted, "military cartridges right here in White County."

"Calm down," the judge said. "Motion denied. Gentlemen, approach the bench, please." He lectured Herman for his little show and the DA seemed relieved it was over, at least for the moment.

"Hang on, boys, it's fixing to get better," Uncle Herman said in a low voice to Jubal and me. "The sheriff has got our best witness on ice in his jail . . . in solitary confinement. But I've got a person inside the jail and I know about it and after lunch all hell's gonna break loose."

Fifteen

"I WANT TO CALL the sheriff back to the stand," Herman said early in the afternoon.

We had heard from two character witnesses already for Jubal, good Caney Fork Baptists who told of his good deeds and said in their estimation he couldn't have done the crime.

"Mr. Sheriff, I want to show you something. It's a summons. I gave this to one of your men and he said he couldn't serve it, said he couldn't find this man anywhere in the county.

"To tell the truth, Sheriff, he's not somewhere out in the county, is he? Truth of the matter, he's in your jail—in solitary confinement, I believe, on a charge of being drunk!"

The DA rolled his eyes and the judge looked disgusted. Herman pressed on, the indignation clear in his voice. "Mr. Sheriff, I want this man in this court in ten minutes. He has vital testimony in this case. I want this summons served on him and I want him delivered to us now."

"Bailiff, go get the prisoner they want. We'll take a short recess," the judge said.

During the break, Herman talked low to Jubal and me and we learned what was going on. At least part of it.

"Remember Sarah?" he asked me. And then for Jubal's benefit, summarized the stabbing case. "Jubal, I got her off pretty light for stabbing her husband. They took her up to Raleigh to serve her time at the women's prison and her teeth were real bad, so the state paid for having her teeth fixed. Now she's physically in pretty good shape, so we petitioned the court to let her serve out her time in the local jail.

"They moved her here to Carverville last week and I was hoping to get her petition heard before this judge, but it hasn't worked out yet. She's the only woman in the jail, so naturally the

155

sheriff and the jailers have got her working in the food end of it. She cooks and serves the food to the men in their cells, then picks up the dishes and washes them. Best jailhouse snitch I've ever had. I have a legitimate right to have conferences with her about her case two or three times a week."

In a few minutes, the witness came in with two deputies and Herman motioned him right to the witness chair beside the judge's bench. "You've been in court before, haven't you?" he asked. "Just not before this particular judge we have today, is that right?"

"You know it is. You've defended me sometimes. I've been here a lot."

"Tell the court, in your own words," Herman said, "what you saw and what you heard when Frog Cutshaw got killed. Nobody told you what to say, have they?"

"No sir, but they put me in jail for no reason. Said I was drunk, but I wasn't. And they put me in the dungeon, by myself."

"Tell the judge what they charge you with when you are usually in court."

"Public drunk, mostly, sometimes for fighting. You got me off one time for fighting, remember that?"

"Yes, I do. You live here in Carverville, don't you?"

"That's right. I ain't no farmer, for sure. I'm a town dude and proud of it. I know ever' street and back alley in town, work a few odd jobs, take a drink once in a while."

"Let's get back to the morning in question. Tell the judge and these men on the jury what happened, what you saw and what sounds you heard."

Dressed in rumpled clothing and badly in need of a shave, the prisoner scratched his head and began to talk, plainly concentrating on giving the details right. "Frog come to town Sunday evening and got me, took me out to his store. Colored boy that worked fer him had run off somewheres, gone he said, and the' wuz a truckload o' t'ars coming in that night would have to be unloaded."

"Black-market tires . . . illegal tires, is that what you mean?"

"I reckon. I heered a lot of talk about Frog selling some t'ars under the table, so to speak, out there but I never asked no questions. He said the driver bringing in the load from Norfolk wouldn't unload it, that was the job I had to do. He wuz gonna pay me five dollars and a pint of whiskey if I would do it."

The witness said he took the task and it was several hours before he had all the tires off the truck, at which point the driver left with the truck. He said he slept on the porch of the store and Cutshaw showed up early Monday morning.

"He said he'd take me back to town and pay me as soon as he got through feeding his hogs," the witness said. "He wanted me to ride down in there with him, wanted me to see a boar hog he called Big Boy, real proud o' that one. But I don't care nothin' about hogs er living out in the country, so I just stayed on the store porch and waited."

"Was anybody else there?"

"No sir, just me. It was kinda foggy. You know how it is real early in the morning. I wanted him to hurry up. I was ready to get back to town."

"So you were the last man to see Frog Cutshaw alive?"

"I reckon so, except for whoever killed him."

Listening to his description, my mind was rolling, taking me back to the spot where Uncle Jubal had fainted and it all looked lost for a few seconds. Then I could remember, plain as day, how that Model 12 felt kicking in my hands, shooting from the hip as Frog Cutshaw glared at me and brought that lethal nickel-plated automatic out from his hip pocket. It seemed so long ago, a memory like Makin Island.

"Tell us what happened, what you heard."

"Well, I could hear good from the store. He drove his truck down into the woods across from the store and I could hear it rattling and beating through the bushes on that rough trail. Then the shooting started. I heard a gun shooting real fast, bout seven er eight times, and the truck never stopped.

"Then in a little bit, the truck stopped, it was real quiet for a minute or so and the shooting started again. I heered a pistol popping, but the main thing was a shotgun went *bam!* about four times in a row, real fast. Then everything was quiet."

"What happened then?" Uncle Herman asked.

The witness said he started toward the scene and some people arrived at the store. He told them what he'd heard and soon dozens of folks were at the hog lot.

"I rode back to town that day with a deputy. I never did get my money er my whiskey from Frog. Reckon I never will."

"Did you consider Mr. Cutshaw a friend?"

"Yes sir, he was okay with me. I just wish he'd lived to pay me."

"You see this gun over on the table. In your opinion, did a gun like that kill Cutshaw, from what you heard on that morning?"

"Objection." the DA said.

"Overruled. The witness can answer the question, giving his own opinion of what he heard at the scene."

"I don't know who shot Frog. But it warn't no turd-kicking farmer with a single-shot gun like that."

"The witness will refrain from gutter language in my court," the judge said, "or I'll have you locked up for contempt."

"I'm already locked up."

"Well, you'll stay longer in jail if you use coarse language again in this room."

The witness took a deep breath, sighed and seemed to pick his words very carefully. "Frog Cutshaw was a deadly man with a pistol. They said the buckshot got him. I reckon it did but the shots I heard that morning come from a shotgun that was a repeater. That's all I got to say."

The DA made a feeble attempt to cross-examine him, but the witness stood firm and was soon sent back to jail.

"Your Honor, I don't know why you're letting some of this go on," the DA said. "We are particularly concerned about the military gun which the defense keeps dragging into the testimony."

Uncle Herman cut him off in mid-sentence, answering the mild objection with a full barrage of verbal overkill. We were very proud of him.

"Your Honor," Herman said, his best formal voice caressing every syllable. "Never in my thirty years of law practice have I seen such a flimsy case against a man on a capital charge. I most certainly hate to say this . . . I know it casts a shadow on the character of the men involved, but I firmly believe in my heart if the victim hadn't been a relative of the sheriff of this county, this case would have never come to trial."

"Objection." The DA's voice cracked into a shrill falsetto. "Move that the last remark be stricken from the record," the DA said hastily.

Grim-faced, the judge ordered Herman and the DA to meet with him in chambers, no assistants allowed.

When Herman came back to the table, he was grinning. "I drew blood that time," he said. "The DA is mad as hell; he's losing control. We're preparing to knock their dick strings in the dirt."

"I thought you told me not to say that anymore."

"Well," he said, "in certain selected cases, I suppose it is appropriate." He stopped grinning two seconds later when the DA rose to speak and asked if the defense was finished.

"Yes sir, I believe we are," Herman answered. Then to me and Jubal, he said real low, "They haven't proved a thing and I'll talk this thing to pieces when I sum it up for the jury."

"We have one more witness we're bringing in tonight from Wilmington," the DA said. "A man who may have something very critical to offer to this trial."

THAT NIGHT, LATER than I thought he would be allowed, I drove Uncle Herman over to the jail and he went in alone. He was carrying a briefcase and a sheaf of papers in his hand, saying he was going to tell the night jailer that he had to meet with Sarah right then.

"I'll tell him we may get Sarah her hearing before the judge tomorrow and I need to confer with her. I might even be telling the truth. When Jubal's case goes to the jury, the judge might be willing to actually hear Sarah's petition."

Of course, he was going to try to find out about the secret witness the DA was bringing in, see what Sarah knew. And I heard all about it when he got back to the car.

"A Wilmington colored man, small-time thief and hustler, told detectives in that city that he bought a repeater shotgun and shells for it for two white women." Herman stared right at me when he said this, looking for a reaction from me. He got none.

"Their police heard about the murder case here and offered their witness as a gesture to our sheriff here. It's really bizarre. It should be part of the investigation, but that's not the way they can handle it now. The DA is going to put this fellow on the witness stand, question him and see if he can identify anyone in the room. Do you suppose he will?"

I shook my head. It was getting deep now, but we could only sit tight and see it through. Aunt Alma in her Sunday best had sat behind Jubal for every day of the trial and would be right there tomorrow. She had hired the negro, she said, and told him not to look at her. But would he identify her? And if he did, where would we go from there?

Herman had smelled a rat since the beginning and I knew it and he knew it. But he had never directly pressed me on it and I wasn't offering anything. We were close to being out of the woods.

Two important things happened the next morning before we went back to the courtroom. One was that I told Uncle Jubal and Aunt Alma what was going to happen.

"Don't matter," Uncle Jubal said. "A colored man's word against a white person won't stand. Alma, you just sit tight, like you been doing. Hold y'r head up high. Herman's gonna beat this thing."

The second thing was that the Wilmington colored man got a little something extra from Sarah when she served the prisoners their breakfast that morning.

"TELL THE COURT about the two women and the gun," the DA said.

"Objection," Uncle Herman said. "Your Honor, I have to object vigorously here. This man has never been in White County to my knowledge, and he cannot know anything relevant to this case."

The judge overruled him and let the DA continue. Aunt Alma sat erect and stiff-lipped behind her man, ready for whatever would come. Two Wilmington detectives who had brought the man sat behind the prosecution's table. Willard's wife, who had been driving the car that day, was three or four rows back.

In a quiet voice, the colored man told his story. He said a big touring car with two white ladies had been parked at the curb and one of the ladies called him over to their car. "I went in a pawn shop, where they had parked real close to it, and I bought a pump shotgun and five buckshots to go in it."

The gun was wrapped in brown paper, he said, and the shells in a little paper poke. The ladies had paid him for his trouble, he said, and then drove away. The DA took a quick look at us and our table and Alma sitting in the front row of the spectators seats right behind us. It was coming now, I could feel it.

"The two white ladies you bought the gun for, the pump 12 gauge shotgun you described, are either one of those ladies in this courtroom? Take your time, nobody is going to hurt you. Tell us if you see either one of those ladies."

Herman objected loudly, saying this should be part of the investigation and not the trial itself. The judge commented that it was a strange trial but he was going to allow the question. The colored man locked eyes with Aunt Alma and I distinctly heard her gasp but she sat straight and never blinked. Finally, he spoke. "No sir, they not here."

"What? Look out over this room and tell me if one of the ladies who bought the shotgun is here?"

"No sir, neither one of 'em is here."

"Are you sure?"

"Yas suh, I am. Besides, all white folks look kinda alike to me."

"What?" The DA was flabbergasted. "All white people look alike to you?"

The witness nodded and the DA hung his head. There was some snickering among the spectators and a couple of the jurymen.

"This is the most insolent colored man I've ever questioned," the DA said when he recovered his composure. "Your witness."

Herman at first looked like he was going to dismiss the man without a word but I saw a gleam in his eye and nudged Jubal, so he wouldn't miss anything.

"You've got a criminal record in Wilmington, don't you?"

"Yas suh, I done a little time for small stuff."

"Tell us, were you out at Caney Fork one morning last September shooting a military carbine at Frog Cutshaw?" Laughter sounded all around the room as the DA leaped to his feet to object.

"Sustained."

The witness was dismissed and taken back to Wilmington that very afternoon, while Herman and the DA made their cases for the jury.

Sarah proudly told me all about it later but Herman never did acknowledge his part . . . how the colored man went home with a crisp new fifty dollar bill hidden in his shoe.

THE COURTROOM WAS packed, with people standing in the aisles for the final drama.

The DA went first and gave it a good try. He hammered on the fact that the body hadn't been robbed, that it was a crime of passion, reminding jurors that Jubal had made a public threat against Cutshaw's life, that Jubal's gun had been fired and his track at the scene.

"The fatal shots may have come from this gun here, maybe from another gun he had," he said. "I believe this man killed Cutshaw and I want you to convict him."

Sounded lame to me. Herman had said several times that

the track was made later, when Jubal visited the hog lot. But he never put Jubal on the stand—he didn't want the DA questioning him.

"Your Honor, I want to renew my motion that this whole thing be dropped. Before I address the jury, I'd like to ask you to dismiss all charges because the prosecution has no case against him."

The judge mulled it over and the courtroom got quiet. It was plain he was considering doing just that, but he finally ruled the other way. "No," he said, "motion denied, continue."

"This is a farce. This whole trial is a joke," Herman said, thundering toward the jury box. "These good men have been made to sit here all week and listen to a bunch of nothing. The prosecution has spun a case out of thin air—hearsay evidence, nothing but rumors, to darken the name of my client.

"A man of God . . . pillar of his community . . . does nothing but help people. And here he stands before you, pleading for justice, accused by the state of this crime of murder in the first degree."

His delivery rolled over every syllable, deliberately pronounced and given emphasis with the resonance of his bass voice. He gestured with his right hand, pointing toward the high ceiling, in a back and forth rhythm which matched the speech cadence. The jury hung on every word and some of them began to sway slightly back and forth with the intensity of the address. They definitely heard every word; whether they believed it or not, we would soon find out.

"We don't for a minute deny that Mr. Frog Cutshaw was shot to death by someone, a person or persons unknown. We do deny with our fullest strength that Jubal Bailey, sitting here before you today, had anything to do with it. Sure, the man was killed. We know that. But we are furious that the DA and his office would try to pin this crime on this innocent man.

"They made a big noise about his poor old club-footed track being found down at that hog lot. Of course it was. He went there to see for himself. Half the county may have been there that morning as spectators; some of you jurymen yourselves may have gone. It's not a crime to walk through the mud at a hog lot and leave a track.

"They also made a big issue over a speech Jubal Bailey made at the store after that poor little girl died, when she'd been mutilated by a coat hanger, they tell me, to make her body give up a baby that may have been fathered by Mr. Cutshaw. I don't know about any of that. We're not here to try Cutshaw. He's dead now. But this is a free country. We have free speech, thank God, and if Jubal Bailey, an upstanding Baptist deacon at Caney Fork, felt moved enough to say what was on his mind then, men, maybe it needed to be said."

"Amen . . . Praise God!" The response came involuntarily from the lips of the Holiness juror.

The judge glared at him, shook his head and motioned for Herman to continue. I nudged Jubal, who seemed hypnotized by Herman's preaching.

"Thank you, Brother." Herman acknowledged the support and bored right in for the ending. "I know y'all all feel the same way I do about this. There's been no evidence that's worth a hill of beans here. My client has been embarrassed by being dragged into court and tried for his very life, for a shooting he didn't commit. And I want to talk just a moment about the gun and then I'll hush and let you get to work.

"Look at his old gun lying there on the table. There's no way it could have fired three or four times in rapid repetition, is there? It's an old single-shooter; it has to be loaded and reloaded by hand, right?

"Witnesses told us—you all heard them—that a flurry of shots were fired by some sort of military gun, then probably four shots from a shotgun plus the dead man's pistol fired, too." He paused for a drink of water and let that sink in.

"You can't tell me this old man's single-shot gun did all the damage. It just did not happen. And remember this when you go into your room to deliberate. The prosecution has not put one eyewitness on the stand that said Jubal Bailey was there doing the shooting that morning.

"He's a farmer. He doesn't claim to be anything else. His

corn needed picking and that's what he was doing. His tenant said he was right there with them all morning, doing his job. If later, he went over there to see the body, that's his business. It's not a crime.

"One more thing, and I want you to think long about this. I hate to say this and some of y'all will smile, I know, but a man's life is at stake here and I think it's important." He was smiling now and the jury hung on every word.

"The Baileys out at the Caney Fork community of our county are good people but you know, and I know, that they're stingy with their money. As the saying goes, they're tight as the bark on a tree.

"That old gun there is a witness, too. It's telling you that Jubal Bailey would not spend the money on a fancy new repeater. It would cost too much. The prosecution lost their case when they tried to hang that on Jubal Bailey.

"I may be lucky just to get paid my full charges on this case." Jurors were grinning now. "A Bailey loves money and they don't spend it foolishly. Think about it, and do the right thing. If Jubal Bailey was sitting on your jury, if you were being tried for your life, Mr. Bailey would treat you right. All we're asking is that you consider all the evidence, or the lack of it, and do what is right. Thank you."

Sixteen

THE JURY KEPT us there for about an hour, but they freed Uncle Jubal. I felt free myself, like I had been acquitted.

Ruby and her bunch came to Uncle Jubal's house a week later and I happened to be there. They had a letter from Reuben. He had a job and they all wanted to go to Baltimore to join him. They wanted money for bus tickets, including Ruby's sister and her kid from Charleston that had made it to Caney Fork.

"My chi'ren know what happened," Ruby said. We had chased them outside so the adults could talk. I was amazed—it was the closest I had ever come to hearing Ruby pronounce an "r". "I tol'em ta hush. Big Ca'vah come up and get 'em if they tell. Said they wuzn't sca'ed, sed th' Big Ca'vah live in a swamp other side o' town, won't come ta Caney Fork."

We sent Ruby and her sister out too, so we could talk.

"We owe her," Jubal said, "and she knows it. Let's pay it, can't be too bad. Send Wes with 'em to town, put them all on the bus." Aunt Alma got some money out of a jar hidden in a closet and we crammed all of them into the coupe, the rumble seat absolutely jammed with colored children. They left on the bus that night, bound for Baltimore.

DARLENE AND I got married in June that year in the First Methodist Church and Felicia sang. There was a good crowd and they were knocked out by her voice, almost forgetting she was a colored woman singing in a white church. Almost.

Turkey Jack showed up for the festivities in his slouch hat with the turkey feather, but he had on a new suit and tie, with a pair of handmade Mexican cowboy boots that dazzled us. I was proud of my partner and the numbers he was producing with the sawmill.

Darlene and I both went to the teachers college up at Greenville and then, when the war ended and they got the GI Bill going, I went on to law school at Chapel Hill and passed the bar exam.

They had a bar association at Carverville, which usually met at the country club where the lawyers did their drinking, and it included attorneys from five surrounding counties.

After I had passed everything else, I would have to join the local bar association. There was a little interview they did at their regular meeting, for any new would-be member. I was nervous, but Herman, who was going to take me into his firm, said it would be easy and very brief.

After everyone had a drink or two, we adjourned to a paneled meeting room and the three senior officers sat down at a table and motioned for me to stand in front of them. It felt like a trial. But all the others were standing, and I could sense that it wouldn't take long—they wanted to get back to the bar.

"Wesley, you've passed all the tests, and Herman's ready to put you to work," the president said. "You must be of good moral character, of course, and therefore we have only one question to ask of you. Son, have you ever killed anyone, taken a human life?"

"Only during World War Two, sir."

He thoughtfully digested my answer, nodded and rose to shake my hand. There was a polite round of applause, and I became an attorney on the spot.

About The Author

Wally Avett is a retired
newspaperman. He lives in North
Carolina.

CPSIA information can be obtained
at www.ICGtesting.com
Printed in the USA
BVOW03s1919111017
497416BV00001B/104/P